ROME. MAY 54. NOON. EMPEROR CLAUDIUS HAS BEEN WATCHING COMBATS SINCE DAWN. THE HEAT IS INTOLERABLE. THE CROWD HAS LEFT TO COOL DOWN OR HAVE LUNCH. CLAUDIUS DOES NOT LEAVE HIS THRONE.

AT THIS TIME OF THE DAY, THE SLAVES WHO SURVIVED THE MORNING COMBATS FIGHT IN THE ARENA. THEIR HALF-NAKED BODIES, ARE NOT OF MUCH INTEREST TO ANYONE. NOBODY MINDS THEIR AGONY.

SMILE. THE EMPEROR IS WAVING TO YOU.

NO. I AM EATING.

BE CAREFUL, OR YOU WILL MAKE HIM LOSE HIS TEMPER.

I HAVE NOTHING MORE TO OFFER. HE TOOK EVERY-THING.

YOUR MOTHER HAD NO CHOICE. I THINK SHE LOVES HIM IN HER OWN WAY. SHE WAS ABLE TO STIR HIM.

MY MOTHER IS FREE TO DO WHAT SHE LIKES. BUT SHE CAN- NOT ASK ME TO SHARE HER PASSIONS.

LOOK!! THREE ARE LEFT!!

TWO!

ONE!! AAAHHH

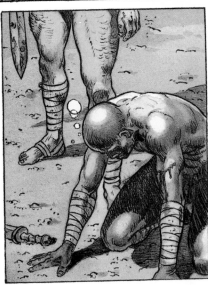

HOC HABET(1) IT'S OVER. LET'S DESCEND.

HIT ME. WHAT ARE YOU WAITING FOR?

I...

HE'S FALLING DOWN! THE NUBIAN IS SAFE!

CAESAR! THIS SLAVE STILL BREATHES!

YES. ISN'T IT SURPRIS- ING?

THEY CLING TO LIFE. IT IS HARD TO LEAVE, EVEN IF YOU ARE NOTHING.

CUT HIS THROAT. I WANT TO HEAR HIS LAST SIGH.

WHAT ABOUT THIS ONE, CAESAR?

OH, YES! THE NUBIAN.

3.

HE WAS LUCKY.

HE SHOULD HAVE DIED.

BUT HE FOUGHT VALIANTLY. I AM DISPOSED TO GRANT HIM PARDON.

YOU, SLAVE, CAESAR IS LISTENING...IMPLORE HIS MERCY!

BRUTE! HOW DARE YOU DEFY THE EMPEROR? YOU SHALL DIE!

NO NO

SAVE HIM, FATHER! I BEG YOU!!!

BRITANNICUS! WHAT... WHAT ARE YOU DOING HERE?

4.

YOUR BROTHER IS WITH YOU, I SEE. WHERE WERE YOU, TWO?

WE HID IN THE CORRIDORS. WE CAME TO SEE THE BLACK FIGHT.

HE IS BRAVE, FATHER. WE HAVE SEEN ALL HIS COMBATS. I BEG YOU TO SAVE HIS LIFE.

SON, I HAVE NOT ALWAYS BEEN FAIR WITH YOU. BECOME AN ADULT AND I WILL MAKE ALL MY ACTIONS CLEAR.

IN THE MEANTIME, TAKE THIS SLAVE. DO WITH HIM WHAT YOU WILL.

LEAVE US, NOW. I WISH TO BE ALONE WITH MY SON.

YOU LOOK PENSIVE.

ARE YOU ALONE? DID YOUR STEP-BROTHER LEAVE YOU?

HE IS WITH YOUR FATHER, ISN'T HE? THEY DO NOT NEED YOU ANYMORE.

IT IS TRUE, YOU ARE THE ONE WHO WAS ADOPTED, NOT BY HEART BUT BY A MOTHER'S AMBITION. AMBITION IS IMPORTANT, ISN'T IT?

YES.

WHAT DO YOU WANT FROM THE WORLD?

THAT IT LISTENS TO ME! AND KNOWS WHAT A GREAT ACTOR AND POET I AM!

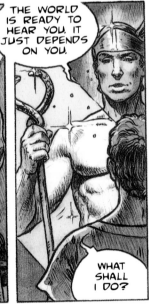

THE WORLD IS READY TO HEAR YOU. IT JUST DEPENDS ON YOU.

WHAT SHALL I DO?

BE AS AMBITIOUS AS THE GODS. DO NOT SUCCUMB TO MAN'S FEARS AND WEAK-NESSES. YOU TOO, YOU SHALL BE A GOD.

IF YOU REALLY WANT TO.

6.

I DESIRE... TO MAKE MY OWN DECISIONS WITHOUT LIMITS.

THEN, THE SACRED FIRE WILL BURN INSIDE YOU AND REACH OLYMPUS, WHERE AMBROSIA AND NECTAR WILL BE POURED IN YOUR HONOR.

GO, LUCIUS DOMITIUS NERO! GLORY AND FORTUNE IS YOURS IF YOU FOLLOW MY LIGHT.

OUR LIGHT.

AND HE SAID, "BECOME AN ADULT AND I WILL MAKE ALL MY ACTIONS CLEAR"?

YES, MISTRESS.

HOW DID MY SON REACT?

HE DID NOT SAY A WORD. HE LEFT ALONE.

HMM. WHAT DO THE COURTESANS SAY ABOUT THAT?

THE TRUTH IS HARD TO ACCEPT, MY MISTRESS.

THE TRUTH, PALLAS. ONLY THE TRUTH.

IT IS SAID YOU WED THE EMPEROR TO MAKE HIM RECOGNIZE YOUR SON. HE ADOPTED HIM AND OPENED THE WAY TO THE THRONE. BUT...

BUT?

IT SEEMS THE EMPEROR FEELS REMORSE FOR THAT. LATE, BUT AUTHENTIC. HE REGRETS HAVING DISREGARDED HIS OWN SON FOR YOURS. SOME COURTESANS ALSO THINK...

NOBODY KNOWS, MISTRESS. FROM TIME TO TIME HE SIMPLY DISAPPEARS. I ASKED MY MEN TO INQUIRE.

...THAT HE COULD CHANGE HIS MIND AGAIN, AS FOR THE SUCCESSION. BRITANNICUS COULD STILL INHERIT THE THRONE.... WHERE IS THE EMPEROR?

AAAHHHHH

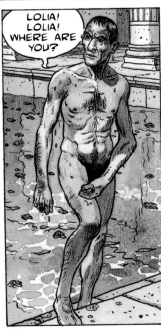

LOLIA! LOLIA! WHERE ARE YOU?

QUICK. I AM COLD.

WHERE WERE YOU?

I WAS WITH MY SON. HE SAW YOU THIS MORNING. HE SAID YOU PARDONED A SLAVE.

8.

YES, THIS IS TRUE. HE DID NOT EVEN DEIGN TO THANK ME.

LOLIA! YOUR SON IS UNDER MY PROTECTION! AS IT IS EVERYTHING THAT BELONGS TO THIS HOUSE. I LOVE YOU LOLIA. YOU SEEM TO FORGET IT, SOMETIMES.

I DO NOT, CLAUDIUS. I DO NOT.

YOU KNOW HE IS A SAVAGE. DO NOT LOSE YOUR TEMPER ABOUT IT.

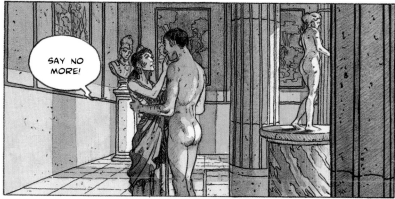

OH LOLIA! HOW CAN YOU DESIRE TO BE WITH A MAN AS UN-ATTRACTIVE AS I AM? I...I WOULD HAVE PREFERRED...

SAY NO MORE!

COME. FOLLOW ME. TONIGHT IS THE NIGHT.

YOUR...YOUR HAIR! WHAT HAPPENED TO IT?

ITS COLOR IS DIFFERENT. AMAZING, ISN'T IT?

YES...YES...I DO NOT UNDERSTAND.

THERE IS NOTHING TO UNDER-STAND! LET'S GO...

10.

CAREFUL! HERE WE ARE!

LOOK, LOOK WHO'S THERE.

MOVE. I WANT TO ENTER

FORGET IT! YOU DIDN'T LEARN ANYTHING LAST TIME?

LAST TIME I WAS ALONE.

SO WHAT? YOUR CREW DOESN'T SCARE ME.

AND I DON'T THINK THE NEW COLOR OF YOUR HAIR MAKES YOU MORE ATTRACTIVE TO THE GIRL. BUT IF YOU WANT, I HAVE A COUPLE OF PALS WHO...

I CHOOSE THE PLEASURE I WANT. AND NOBODY HOLDS ME BACK!!

I...I CANNOT.

FOR THE GODS' SAKE! THEY ARE KILLING EACH OTHER.

YOU'RE DEAD!

AAAAH!

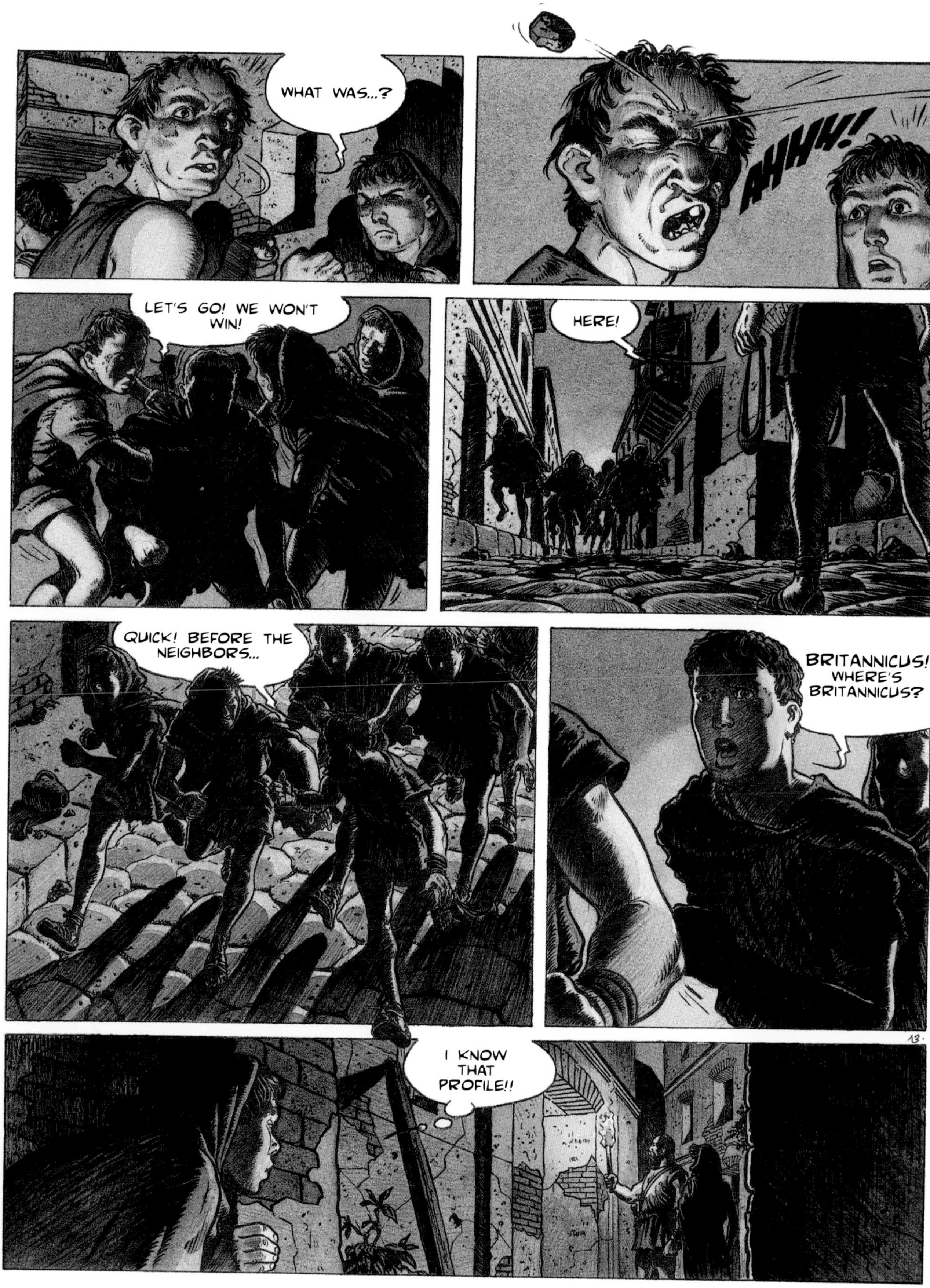
WHAT WAS...?
AHHH!
LET'S GO! WE WON'T WIN!
HERE!
QUICK! BEFORE THE NEIGHBORS...
BRITANNICUS! WHERE'S BRITANNICUS?
I KNOW THAT PROFILE!!
13.

WAIT HERE.

AGRIPPINA!!

OH! IT IS YOU, MISTRESS! I WAS WORRIED...

IS IT READY?

IT IS. FOLLOW ME, MISTRESS.

HIS NAME IS ASPER.

HE KNOWS HE IS ABOUT TO DIE.

DRINK!

I...

DRINK, SLAVE!

LET'S WAIT, NOW.

LOOK!!

15.

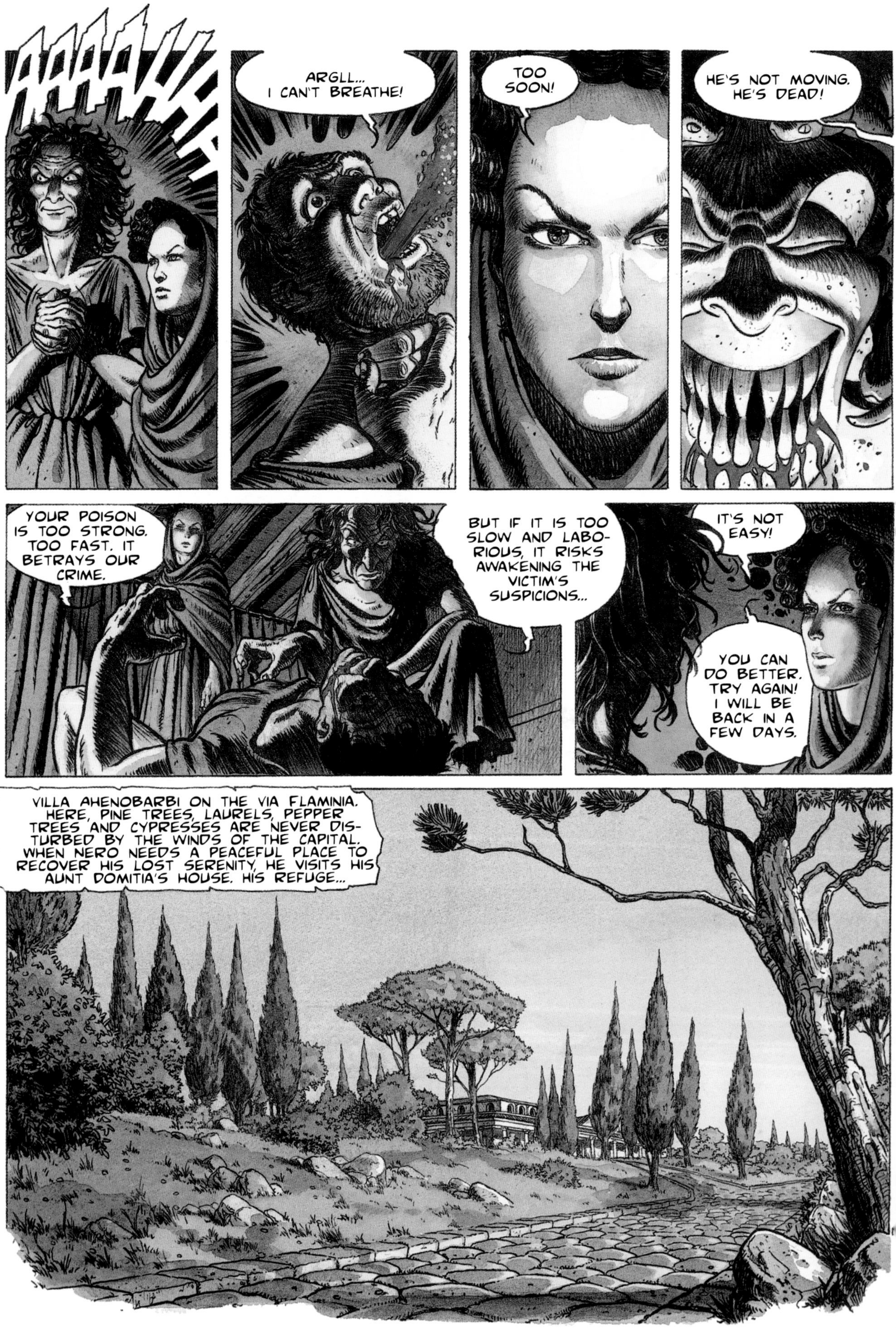
AAAAHH
ARGLL... I CAN'T BREATHE!
TOO SOON!
HE'S NOT MOVING. HE'S DEAD!
YOUR POISON IS TOO STRONG. TOO FAST. IT BETRAYS OUR CRIME.
BUT IF IT IS TOO SLOW AND LABORIOUS, IT RISKS AWAKENING THE VICTIM'S SUSPICIONS...
IT'S NOT EASY!
YOU CAN DO BETTER. TRY AGAIN! I WILL BE BACK IN A FEW DAYS.
VILLA AHENOBARBI ON THE VIA FLAMINIA. HERE, PINE TREES, LAURELS, PEPPER TREES AND CYPRESSES ARE NEVER DISTURBED BY THE WINDS OF THE CAPITAL. WHEN NERO NEEDS A PEACEFUL PLACE TO RECOVER HIS LOST SERENITY, HE VISITS HIS AUNT DOMITIA'S HOUSE. HIS REFUGE...

...BUT NOT FOR LONG!

LUCIUS DOMITIUS...YOUR MOTHER LEFT ROME TO COME AND SEE YOU.

OH!

TO WHAT I OWE THIS HONOR?

I DO NOT KNOW.

YOU DON'T TRUST HER...

LUCIUS, WHEN YOUR FATHER DIED, YOUR MOTHER HAD LITTLE TIME FOR YOU. SHE GAVE YOU TO ME. I'M SURE SHE DOESN'T REGRET THAT I CARED FOR YOU AS IF YOU WERE MY OWN.. NOW, TIMES HAVE CHANGED...

WITH NO FATHER, NO WEALTH, ABANDONED BY EVERYONE, YOU WOULD HAVE BECOME AN ORDINARY BOY, IF YOUR MOTHER HAD NOT BEEN AMBITIOUS. SHE LOVES POWER. IT DOES NOT LEAVE MUCH ROOM FOR ANYTHING ELSE...

MY MOTHER SCARES ME. SHE INTIMIDATES ME. SHE MAKES ME FEEL NERVOUS. I FEEL SHE DOES NOT LOVE ME.

SHE LOVES YOU IN HER OWN WAY...WHICH DIFFERS FROM MINE. I LIKE HOLDING YOU IN MY ARMS. SHE WANTS TO SEE YOU ON A THRONE.

"BUT SHE WON. SHE MARRIED THE EMPEROR. NOW SHE CAN HAVE ALL SHE DESIRES AND HER DESIRES ARE BOUNDLESS!"

THE EMPEROR HAS A SON FROM HIS PREVIOUS MARRIAGE BRITANNICUS[2]. HE IS THE LEGITIMATE HEIR. THEY WILL LEAVE ME ALONE. I ASK NOTHING OF THEM.

YOU ARE MY TRUE MOTHER. I DO NOT WANT TO LEAVE YOU. MAKE ME STAY HERE.

WHAT A LOVELY PICTURE! ONE COULD EASILY BE DECEIVED...

MY APOLOGIES FOR INTERRUPTING!

YOU'RE HERE! I...I DIDN'T HEAR YOU COME!

DO NOT BE WORRIED. I CAME TO SEE MY SON. I WILL BRING HIM BACK TO ROME. HOWEVER, I WOULD LIKE TO TALK TO YOU FIRST...

PLEASE, LEAVE US, LUCIUS DOMITIUS. PREPARE YOUR THINGS.

NO! NOT LUCIUS DOMITIUS!

I DON'T WANT TO HEAR THAT NAME EVER AGAIN. HIS NAME HAS CHANGED SINCE HE WAS ADOPTED BY THE EMPEROR! NOW HE IS TIBERIUS CLAUDIUS NERO. HE IS NOW A CLAUDIAN[3].

I'M NOT ANNOYED THOUGH. HE IS NOT YOUR CONCERN...

WHAT DO YOU MEAN?

THIS IS THE LAST TIME YOU SEE MY SON. YOU HAVE BEEN A LOYAL FAMILY FOR HIM. I SHALL NOT FORGET THAT, BUT NOW, THE COURT IS HIS PLACE. A GREAT FUTURE AWAITS HIM. HE CANNOT BE DISTRACTED...

HERE, HE GETS SOFT. HIS HEART NEEDS TO BE STRONG.

HIS HEART? YOU SPEAK ABOUT HEART, AGRIPPINA? THEN, YOU KNOW WHAT IT IS!

BE CERTAIN...MINE BEATS, TOO! BUT TO THE RHYTHM THAT I HAVE IMPOSED TO IT. AND IT HAS NO RIGHT TO SPEAK!

"WE LEAVE, TIBERIUS CLAUDIUS NERO!"

GOOD LUCK, MY BOY! MAY THE GODS WATCH OVER YOU...

GOODBYE, AUNT. I LOVE YOU, REMEMBER ME.

NOOOOOOOOO

THE PAIN IS EASING...

AAAHH!!

NOT HER! NOT HER! GO AWAY, DEMON!! LEAVE ME ALONE!!!

STEADY, MY SON! YOUR FATHER IS HERE...

I BELIEVE THE CRISIS IS OVER. YOU CAN LEAVE NOW.

FATHER! FATHER! THE HOUSE...I HAVE SEEN IT.... SHE WENT INSIDE.... SHE SPOKE TO HER.... GORGON[4].

WHO WENT INSIDE? WHAT DO YOU MEAN?

POISON OOZED FROM HER MOUTH....SHE SAID YOUR NAME, FATHER....IT IS IN MY DREAM.

HE'S DELIRIOUS...

20

POISON... AND SHE SAID MY NAME...SHE... WHO IS SHE?

OH!

LUCIUS MURENA! WHAT ARE YOU DOING HERE?

SOMEONE UNKNOWN SUMMONED ME, CAESAR.

YOU DO NOT KNOW? HOW BIZARRE! I HOPED YOU TOOK THE TROUBLE TO SEE ME.... APPARENTLY, I AM ILL-FATED. I GREETED YOU YESTERDAY AT THE GAMES, DO YOU REMEMBER?

I WAS WATCHING THE GAMES IN THE BEASTIARIES...(5)

I...I DON'T REMEMBER, CAESAR.

SO...THERE'S NO ROOM FOR ME IN YOUR MEMORIES. A PITY. GIVE MY REGARDS TO YOUR MOTHER. I'LL SEE YOU AGAIN, I THINK...

YES, CAESAR.

HIS MOTHER! HMMM...

HEY!

IT'S ME! COME HERE...

LET'S GO TO MY APARTMENT. WE'LL BE ABLE TO TALK FREELY THERE.

YOU SAVED MY LIFE, LAST NIGHT. WHY? YOU RECOGNIZED ME?

NO. IT WAS TOO DARK. I JUST ACTED ON INSTINCT.

AND SKILL. YOU ARE GOOD WITH THE SLING.

TELL ME, WHAT WERE YOU DOING THERE? DO YOU KNOW THAT HOUSE, THE ONE WITH THE GUARD?

YES. ALL ROMANS KNOW IT.

REALLY? I WONDER WHY...

WAS TOLD A SLAVE GIVES OF HERSELF INSIDE THAT HOUSE. SHE'S VERY BEAUTIFUL AND NO MAN, OR WOMAN CAN SATISFY HER.

IT'S ALSO SAID...

YES?

...THAT AN IMPORTANT MAN OF THE COURT PROTECTS HER AND SELLS HER SEXUAL FAVORS...NOT TO JUST ANYONE, THOUGH...NOT EVEN TO...

...TO THE SON OF THE EMPEROR.

AND IF I WANT TO SEE HER... WOULD YOU HELP ME?

I CAN TELL YOU HER NAME... ACTE.

ACTE...

...HAS BEEN ANNOUNCED THAT A SWARM OF BEES HAS SETTLED ON TOP OF THE CAPITOLIAN JUPITER TEMPLE.

AND IN THE FIELD OF MARS, THE TOMB OF DRUSUS, YOUR FATHER, CAESAR, HAS BEEN HIT BY LIGHTNING.

I WAS INFORMED ABOUT THE BIRTH OF NUMEROUS MISSHAPEN CHILDREN IN DIFFERENT DISTRICTS OF THE CITY.

A SOW GAVE BIRTH TO A BOAR WITH CLAWS AS BIG AS A SPARROW-HAWK'S.

A PRAETOR AND AN OFFICIAL HAVE BEEN MURDERED!

THE ONE WHO INFLICTED THE WOUND MUST NOW HEAL IT...

I MADE A MISTAKE. NEVER, NEVER SHOULD I HAVE REMARRIED THAT WOMAN.

AGRIPPINA AND HER SON DOMINATE MY LIFE. I NEED TO BREATHE. I NEED TO BE ALONE.

BUT HER SON IS YOURS TOO, NOW, CAESAR! YOU HAVE ADOPTED HIM.

HE IS, BUT THIS MADE ME NEGLECT MY OWN SON...MY BRITANNICUS.

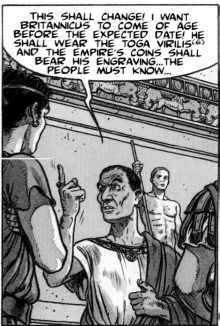

THIS SHALL CHANGE! I WANT BRITANNICUS TO COME OF AGE BEFORE THE EXPECTED DATE! HE SHALL WEAR THE TOGA VIRILIS[6] AND THE EMPIRE'S COINS SHALL BEAR HIS ENGRAVING...THE PEOPLE MUST KNOW...

...THAT HE WILL BE MY SUCCESSOR, WHEN MY TIME COMES.

OUCH! YOU HURT ME!!

PARDON, MISTRESS! I WAS DISTRACTED.

DISTRACTED! I DO NOT LIKE WHEN MY SLAVES LOSE THEIR HEAD! PUT HER UNDER WATER UNTIL I ORDER HER RELEASE.

MISTRESS! FORGIVE ME!!... I...

AFRANIUS BURRHUS WAS PRESENT, TOO?

YES. THE HEAD OF THE PRAETORIUM IS PRESENT AT ALL COUNCILS.

MAKE HIM COME HERE. I HAVE SEEN HIM AT THE SUDATORIUM(?).

MISTRESS? WHAT SHALL WE DO?

OH YES! THE SLAVE...YOU CAN LET HER OUT NOW.

SHE... DOESN'T MOVE! SHE'S DEAD!!

WHAT? PULL HER OUT, BEFORE SHE POLLUTES THE WATERS! MOVE!!

THE EMPRESS WANTS TO SEE YOU.

NOW? I'M COMING.

HE'S HERE.

GOOD! LET HIM IN.

LEAVE US. NOBODY MUST DISTURB US.

FOR YOUR SON TO BE EMPEROR, YOU'LL NEED THE SUPPORT OF THE PRAETORIAN COHORTS. OTHERWISE, YOU'LL BE POWERLESS.

I KNOW. THIS IS WHY I ASKED YOU TO COME.

SIT HERE, NEXT TO ME. WHAT I NEED TO TELL YOU IS EXTREMELY IMPORTANT.

LET ME GUESS. YOU NEED MY HELP TO BETRAY CAESAR...MY MASTER...YOUR SPOUSE...

POOR MASTER... POOR SPOUSE, WHO'S NOT EVEN ABLE TO SATISFY ME NOR DOES HE SATISFY HIS EMPIRE... DO NOT DENY THAT. YOU AGREE WITH ME.

AND YOUR SON? WILL HE BE BETTER? WHO CAN GUARANTEE THAT?

I CAN! I WILL BE THE POWER AND HE WILL BE ITS FACE.

YOU NEED A MAN ON THE THRONE. YOU WILL HAVE IT! BUT IT WILL BE MY SEX THAT WILL TRIUMPH. AND I WANT YOU TO BE PART OF THIS TRIUMPH...

15,000 SESTERCES FOR EACH PRAETORIAN. FREE DISTRIBUTION OF ADDITIONAL WHEAT EVERY MONTH. A NEW COLONY FOR THE VETERAN SOLDIERS.

AND YOU WILL PERSONALLY INTRODUCE YOUR SON TO THE CASTRA PRAETORIA (8), WEARING PURPLE AND PRECEDED BY LICTORS. HE WILL BE THE NEW HEAD OF THE ARMY.

I WILL FOLLOW YOUR ADVICE. AND NOW, QUICK. WHAT EXPECTS US CANNOT BE DELAYED FURTHER.

I HAVE DECIDED TO MARRY YOU!

WHAT!!? BUT... THE EMPRESS??

SHE WILL NEVER LET YOU RENOUNCE HER. WE DISCUSSED THIS.

YES. BUT TIMES HAVE CHANGED. NOW, IT IS ME OR HER!

REMEMBER, BEFORE I EVEN MET AGRIPPINA, I WANTED YOU TO BE MY SPOUSE.

BUT IT WAS HER THAT YOU CHOSE TO HAVE BY YOUR SIDE.

THIS WAY,
BE CAREFUL!
MAKE NO
NOISE.

THERE! I
TOLD
YOU!

HER! I
KNEW IT. THE
SON LED ME TO
HIS MOTHER, AND
HIS MOTHER LED
ME TO THE
EMPEROR. NOW
I HAVE SOMETHING
TO
NEGOTIATE!

REMEMBER I WAS CHASING
YOU AND YOU FELL DOWN.
YOU HIT YOUR HEAD
AGAINST THIS FOUNTAIN.

I WAS
JUST A GIRL.
I LOST
TWO TEETH,
THAT DAY.

I KNOW. I FELT SO
GUILTY ABOUT THAT. I
THINK OF IT EVERY
TIME I KISS YOU.

YOU WILL NOT FORGET
MY SON, WILL YOU?

I WILL NOT.
YOU HAVE
MY WORD.

GIVE HIM HIS MONEY!
HE DESERVED IT. BUT
DON'T SAY A WORD,
OR I'LL...

I WILL
BE AS
SILENT AS
THE GRAVE.

HA, HA. THIS WAS A GOOD DEAL.

SO, YOUR TRADE IS FLOURISHING!

?!?

WHO WERE THESE PEOPLE? WHAT DID THEY WANT FROM YOU?

THESE PEOPLE? ER...THEY WERE JUST FRIENDS, MASTER.

THEY WERE? SO WHY SHOULD A SLAVE INVITE HIS FRIENDS TO MY HOUSE, THEN?

THIS IS THE FIRST TIME, MASTER.

EAT!

WHAT?

THE COINS YOU RECEIVED. SWALLOW THEM ONE AFTER THE OTHER, UNTIL YOU ANSWER MY QUESTIONS! AGREED?

??

OR I'LL CUT YOUR THROAT RIGHT HERE!

ONE BY ONE, SLAVE.

SOME FRIENDS, MY MASTER. JUST FRIENDS.

GLPPP...

FASTER, SLAVE.

I HAVE NO TIME TO WASTE!

QUICK! EMPTY YOUR BAG!!

GOOD. KEEP AT IT... ONE MORE...

MERCY, MASTER...MY THROAT IS IN TATTERS...

WHO WERE THEY? WHAT DID THEY WANT?

PALLAS... IT WAS HIM AT THE DOORS OF YOUR DWELLING. HE WANTED TO SEE YOUR MOTHER...TO SEE IF SHE KNOWS ANYONE OF THE COURT... HE JUST WANTED TO SEE HER...NOTHING MORE.

PALLAS!!!

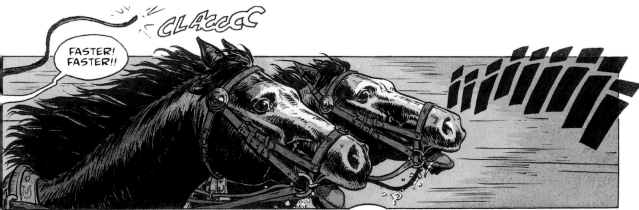

CLASSS

FASTER! FASTER!!

STOP!!

SO?

SUPERB! YOUR BEST RACE EVER!!

YOU'LL WIN. YOU WILL!!

HE IS REALLY A GREAT RACER. WHAT DO YOU THINK?

HIS STRENGTH IS REAL.

BUT I KNOW SOMEBODY WHO COULD BEAT HIM.

MY BROTHER? IMPOSSIBLE! ANYONE WHO DOES WILL BE BEHEADED.

BETTER TO LOSE YOUR LIFE THAN YOUR PRIDE.

YOU ARE A STRANGE SLAVE! SOMETIMES YOU SCARE ME...AND SOME-TIMES...

HMM...?

...I FEEL I CAN TRUST YOU--THAT YOU ARE SINCERE.

YOU SAVED ME, I WON'T FORGET THAT.

34

CAREFUL ABOUT ORESTE. HE WILL LEAD TWO THESSALONIAN MARES. THEY RUN FASTER.

ONCE YOU REACH THE CURVE YOU'LL NEED TO GET IN HIS WAY. HE ALWAYS RUNS AT THE RIGHT OF THE STELE AND MAKES HIS AXLE SURFACE.

CORRECT! DURING THE LAST RACE HE RISKED BREAKING THE HUB. HE MADE UP GROUND ONLY AT THE LAST MOMENT.

I NEED TO TALK TO YOU.

OH--IT'S YOU! WHAT HAP-PENED? YOU LOOK SERIOUS.

THERE IS A REA-SON FOR THAT. COME...

MY MOTHER IS IN DANGER. I NEED TO KNOW IF I CAN COUNT ON YOU.

HOW COME? TELL ME...

PALLAS SPIES ON MY HOUSE. HE SAW MY MOTHER WITH THE EMPEROR.

REALLY? I DIDN'T KNOW SHE WAS ONE OF HIS MANY MISTRESSES.

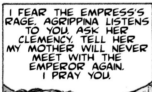

I FEAR THE EMPRESS'S RAGE, AGRIPPINA LISTENS TO YOU. ASK HER CLEMENCY. TELL HER MY MOTHER WILL NEVER MEET WITH THE EMPEROR AGAIN. I PRAY YOU.

THAT THE EMPEROR CHEATS ON MY MOTHER DOESN'T BOTHER ME. IT'S HER PROBLEM, BUT SHE COULD BE JEAL-OUS...AND VINDICTIVE. THIS DEPENDS ON PALLAS' REPORT...

!?!

BEWARE. DON'T TRUST PALLAS. TONIGHT, YOU'LL KNOW WHY.

32.

LOOK!

RECOGNIZE HIM? THE ONE HOLDING THE TORCH.

IT'S HIM! THEN...THEN...

YES...ACTE IS IN THE LITTER. WHEN SHE IS NOT BUSY SELLING HER FAVORS, SHE COMES HERE TO BATHE. ALWAYS ON THE SAME BANK...SAFE FROM PRYING EYES... EXCEPT OURS.

ACTE...

WHERE ARE WE GOING?

QUIET, WE'RE HERE!

33.

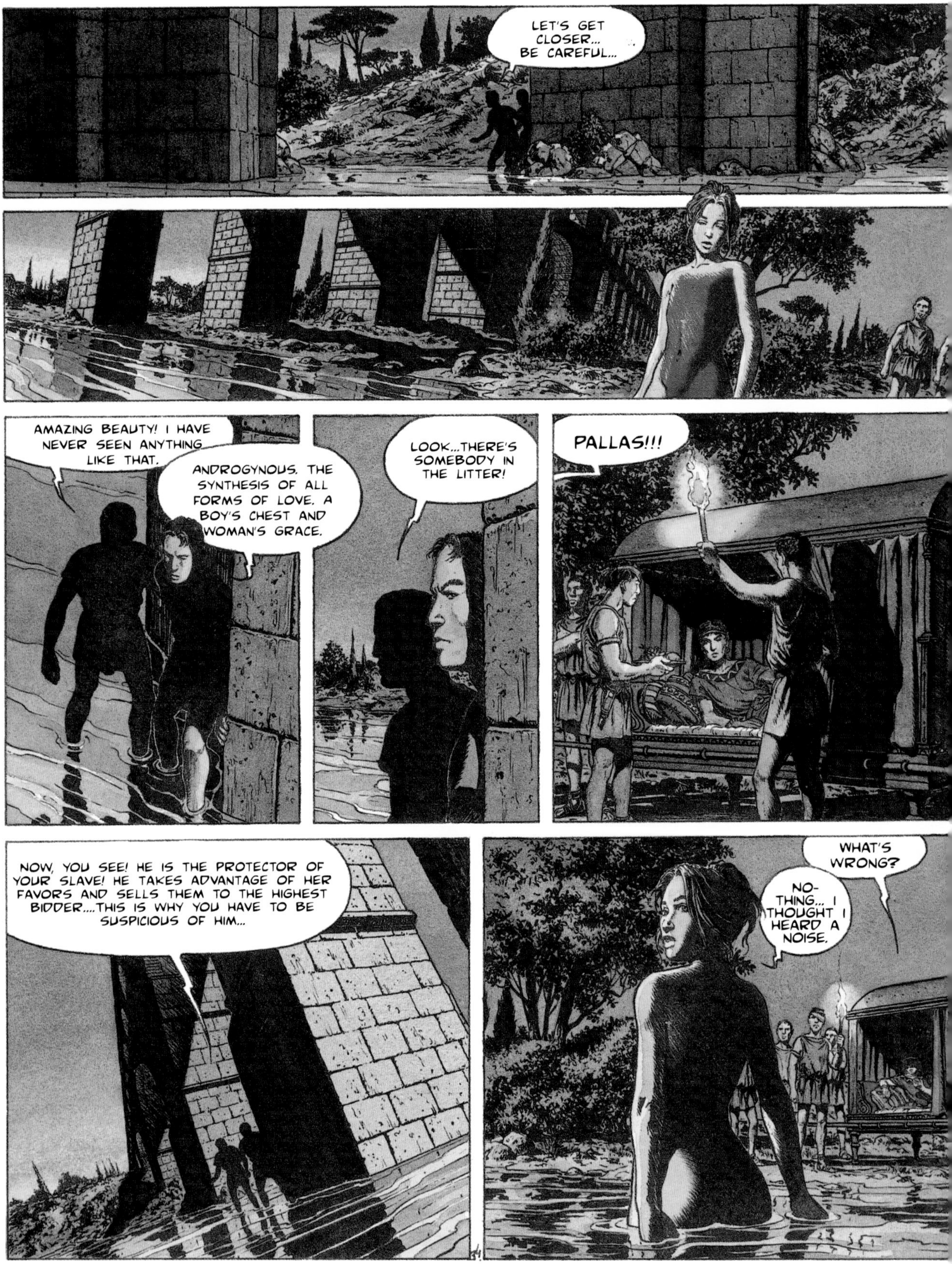
LET'S GET CLOSER... BE CAREFUL...
AMAZING BEAUTY! I HAVE NEVER SEEN ANYTHING LIKE THAT.
ANDROGYNOUS. THE SYNTHESIS OF ALL FORMS OF LOVE. A BOY'S CHEST AND WOMAN'S GRACE.
LOOK...THERE'S SOMEBODY IN THE LITTER!
PALLAS!!!
NOW, YOU SEE! HE IS THE PROTECTOR OF YOUR SLAVE! HE TAKES ADVANTAGE OF HER FAVORS AND SELLS THEM TO THE HIGHEST BIDDER....THIS IS WHY YOU HAVE TO BE SUSPICIOUS OF HIM...
WHAT'S WRONG?
NO-THING... I THOUGHT I HEARD A NOISE.

DO THE SENATORS REMEMBER HOW CLAUDIUS CAME INTO POWER?

HIDING BEHIND CURTAINS AND AFRAID TO BE SEEN WHILE HIS FAMILY WAS BEING MASSACRED. HE LEFT HIS HIDING PLACE ONLY WHEN A SOLDIER SAW HIS FEET APPEARING UNDER THE DRAPES⁽⁹⁾.

HE WAS THE ONLY ONE LEFT. NOBODY ELSE COULD HAVE CLAIMED THE VACANT THRONE. HE CAME OUT STAMMERING, FALTERING, SNOTTY.

AND THE SOLDIERS PROCLAIMED HIM EMPEROR! THE FIRST CAESAR TO GAIN HIS LAUREL BY MEANS OF FORCE, INSTEAD OF OUR FATHERS' WISDOM.

THIS IS THE MAN WHO IS GOVERNING US. ALWAYS STAMMERING AND FALTERING, WHETHER HE'S RULING OUR COUNTRY OR SLIPPING INTO MY BED.

YOUR WORDS ARE HARSH.

35.

AFTER ALL, THE SENATE HAS NOTHING TO REPROACH YOUR SPOUSE.

YOU AND YOUR FRIENDS CAN CHANGE THIS. FOR EXAMPLE, I KNOW THAT NUMEROUS SENATORS BELONGING TO WEALTHY FAMILIES WERE RUINED.

WE CAN REMEDY THAT WITH ANNUAL PAYMENTS.

HOW MUCH?

500,000 SESTERCES. BUT FOR YOU, I HAVE DIFFERENT PLANS...

THE COMBAT IS OVER. THEY AWAIT YOUR DECISION...

YES! THE THRACIAN LOST... KILL HIM! HE WILL BE GOOD AT DYING.

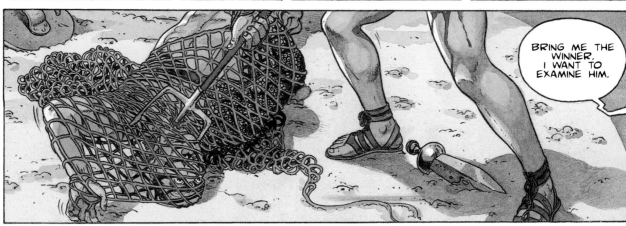

BRING ME THE WINNER. I WANT TO EXAMINE HIM.

FOR YOU, THE PRAETORSHIP AND MUCH MORE. I WANT YOU TO EDUCATE OUR NEW CAESAR. YOU SHALL BE HIS MENTOR.

AH! AND WHO'S OUR NEW CAESAR?

MY SON LUCIUS DOMITIUS NERO.

HMM! FOR HIM TO BECOME EMPEROR, CAESAR MUST DIE. AND WE MIGHT WAIT TOO LONG FOR THAT TO HAPPEN.

I DON'T LIKE WAITING. YOU SHOULD KNOW THAT.

MY SON. YOU WISH TO SEE ME?

WE NEED TO TALK.

CERTAINLY. BUT, FIRST LET ME INTRODUCE YOU TO YOUR MENTOR.

SENECA WILL BE YOUR PRECEPTOR. HE HAS MY TRUST.

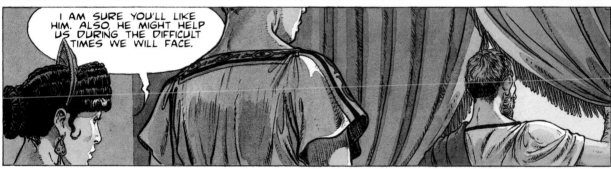

I AM SURE YOU'LL LIKE HIM. ALSO, HE MIGHT HELP US DURING THE DIFFICULT TIMES WE WILL FACE.

WHO...? OH! ENTER.

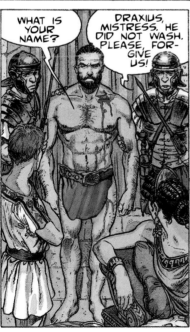

WHAT IS YOUR NAME?

DRAXIUS, MISTRESS. HE DID NOT WASH. PLEASE, FORGIVE US!

NO NO...THIS IS WHAT I LIKE. SMELLING HIS ROUGHNESS, HIS STRENGTH...

...HIS BLOOD. LEAVE US. I WILL SPEAK TO HIM ALONE... NOT YOU MY SON. YOU CAN STAY.

37

I HAVE BEEN WATCHING YOU FOR SOME TIME, DRAXIUS. YOU ARE VALIANT. YOU DESERVE YOUR VICTORIES.

WOULD YOU LIKE YOUR FREEDOM? I HAVE A PROPOSAL FOR YOU.

I'M LISTENING.

A WOMAN DARED TO HUMILIATE ME. BRING ME HER HEAD AND YOU WILL BE FREE. HER NAME IS LOLIA PAULINA. I WILL TELL YOU WHERE SHE IS AND WHEN YOU CAN SOLVE THE MATTER.

?!?

MOTHER! WHY DO YOU BLAME HER? PERHAPS YOU HEARD SOME RUMORS...

RUMORS! WHAT PALLAS REPORTS HAS NOTHING TO DO WITH RUMORS. IT IS THE TRUTH.

CLAUDIUS HAS BECOME INFATUATED WITH HER! HE IS EVEN THINKING ABOUT MARRYING HER. I SHOULD NOT REACT? IS THAT YOUR SUGGESTION, MY SON?

LOLIA PAULINA IS THE MOTHER OF ONE OF MY FRIENDS. PLEASE, MOTHER...EXILE OR BANISH HER, BUT DO NOT KILL HER!

ALSO, I MUST TELL YOU ABOUT PALLAS! HE IS NOT TO BE TRUSTED! DID YOU KNOW HE CORRUPTS YOUR GIRLS? AND HE PROFITS FROM IT!

WELL... SHOULD I CARE? HE CAN TAKE PLEASURE OR MAKE MONEY OUT OF WHATEVER HE LIKES.

I CARE! I...I WANT ONE OF THOSE GIRLS! BUT I DO NOT HAVE THE MONEY FOR THAT!

LISTEN TO THIS! ARE YOU IN LOVE, MY SON? YOU APPEAR PROUD ENOUGH TO SUFFER FROM WHAT IS UNJUSTLY IMPOSED TO YOU...SO AM I!

BE ASSURED, MY SON. WE WILL NOT ENDURE THIS HUMILIATION! I WILL TALK TO PALLAS. THE GIRL WILL BE YOURS.

AS LOLIA WILL BE MINE, RIGHT?

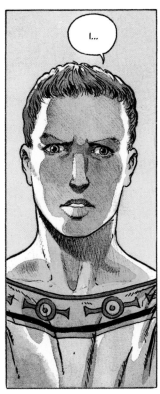

I...

ON THE NIGHT OF OCTOBER 12, WHILE COURTSANS PREPARE FOR THE ANNUAL CELEBRATIONS IN HONOR OF DIVINE AUGUST, ANIMAL LIVERS ARE SCATTERED ON THE GROUND, THE ULTIMATE SIGN FOR ILL WILL. A FATEFUL SIGN, LIKE THE DARK CLOUDS GATHERING OVER THE CITY. NOTHING GOOD WILL HAPPEN THIS NIGHT.

YOU MUST ATTEND! THE SON OF AGRIPPINA HAS INVITED YOU PERSONALLY. THINK ABOUT YOUR FUTURE. THIS IS A CHANCE TO BE ADMITTED TO THE COURT.

I KNOW. BUT...

I DO NOT WANT TO LEAVE YOU, TONIGHT. I'M WORRIED.

WHY, MY DARLING? YOU FORGET, THE EMPEROR PROTECTS US.

NOTHING CAN HAPPEN, BELIEVE ME. DO NOT FEAR. GO AND ENJOY. YOU WILL TELL ME EVERYTHING ABOUT OUT IT, WHEN YOU RETURN.

THERE HE IS! LET HIM LEAVE BEFORE WE ATTACK. THOSE ARE THE ORDERS!

REMEMBER! NO WITNESSES!!

BE STRONG, MY SON. THE WORLD WILL OFFER YOU ANY GIFTS. TAKE ALL YOU CAN BEFORE YOU ARE TAKEN.

I HAVE PREPARED THE ACT OF REJECTION. AGRIPPINA WILL LEAVE US SOON. YOU ARE MY ONLY HEIR, SON.

AND NERO, FATHER? I...I DO NOT WANT HIM TO GRIEVE.

YOUR STEPBROTHER WILL GO WITH HER INTO EXILE. HE SHOULD FEEL BLESSED.

I WILL PROCLAIM MY DECISION TO THE SENATE TOMORROW. YOU MUST ATTEND. THEY MUST ACCLAIM YOU AS YOU DESERVE.

I...I WILL TRY TO BE WORTHY, FATHER.

LET'S GO CELEBRATE, NOW. I RECOVERED MY APPETITE. HALOTHAS THE EUNUCH TASTED MY DISHES. HE TOLD ME WE WILL HAVE MUSHROOMS, TONIGHT!

I KNOW YOU LOVE THEM, FATHER.

WHERE IS HE? I TOLD HIM THERE ISN'T MUCH TIME LEFT!!!

MAYBE HE ENCOUNTERED UNEXPECTED RESISTANCE.

SOMEONE KNOCKED! ENTER!

HERE I AM...AND HERE IS WHAT YOU WANTED.

"WE WERE QUICK AND MET WITH NO RESISTANCE..."

41

"...EXCEPT FOR AN OLD CLUMSY MAN WHO TRIED TO GRAB A SWORD. BUT HE WAS NOT A PROBLEM."

"THEN, I TOOK CARE OF THE WOMAN PERSONALLY."

IS IT HER?

LOLIA PAULINA!

HOW CAN WE BE CERTAIN?

HER TEETH, MISTRESS...LET ME EXAMINE HER TEETH.

OPEN HER MOUTH, I WILL CHECK.

THIS IS HER! THE TEETH ARE ODD DUE TO AN OLD FALL(10).

WHAT!!? WHAT'S WRONG? YOU LOOK AS IF YOU'D SEEN...?

A MEDUSA'S HEAD, YES...

THE... THE SAME OMEN! IT OPPRESSES ME...

THE DISH...BRING THE DISH.

MUSHROOMS. PERFECT.

DONE! THE EFFECT WILL NOT BE IMMEDIATE. BE SURE HE IS THE ONLY ONE SERVED FROM THIS PLATE.

43

AH! MY FAVORITE!

EAT, MY FRIENDS, EAT. LET'S SURRENDER TO THE LAW OF THE BANQUET TONIGHT!

I DO NOT SEE YOUR SON...

MY SON? HE IS YOUR SON TOO, CAESAR. DON' FORGET THAT.

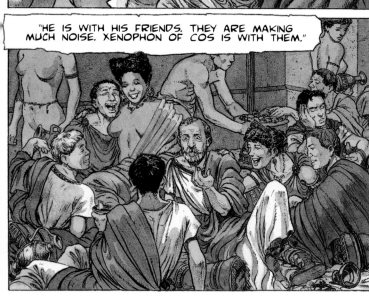

"HE IS WITH HIS FRIENDS. THEY ARE MAKING MUCH NOISE. XENOPHON OF COS IS WITH THEM."

SO, LUCIUS, WHY DO YOU LOOK SO PENSIVE? WE ARE NOT AN AMUSING COMPANY FOR YOU?

YOU ARE...

IT IS PALLAS' PRESENCE THAT TROUBLES ME. LOOK HOW HE IS PARADING IN FRONT OF THE EMPRESS. I SHALL NOT BE HAPPY UNTIL HE IS GONE FROM THE COURT.

YOU REMEMBER YOUR PROMISE, DON'T YOU? DID YOU TALK TO YOUR MOTHER?

YES... I...

SHE WILL SEE WHAT SHE CAN DO.

THANK YOU. I WILL NEVER FORGET WHAT I OWE YOU.

LOOK! CAESAR! HE IS FEELING SICK! HE IS ABOUT TO VOMIT.

HE STUFFED HIM-SELF, THE OLD MAN! THAT'S NOT THE FIRST TIME!

I...I'M HOT! I CAN-NOT BREATHE! I MUST GO OUT...

OOOHHH!

45

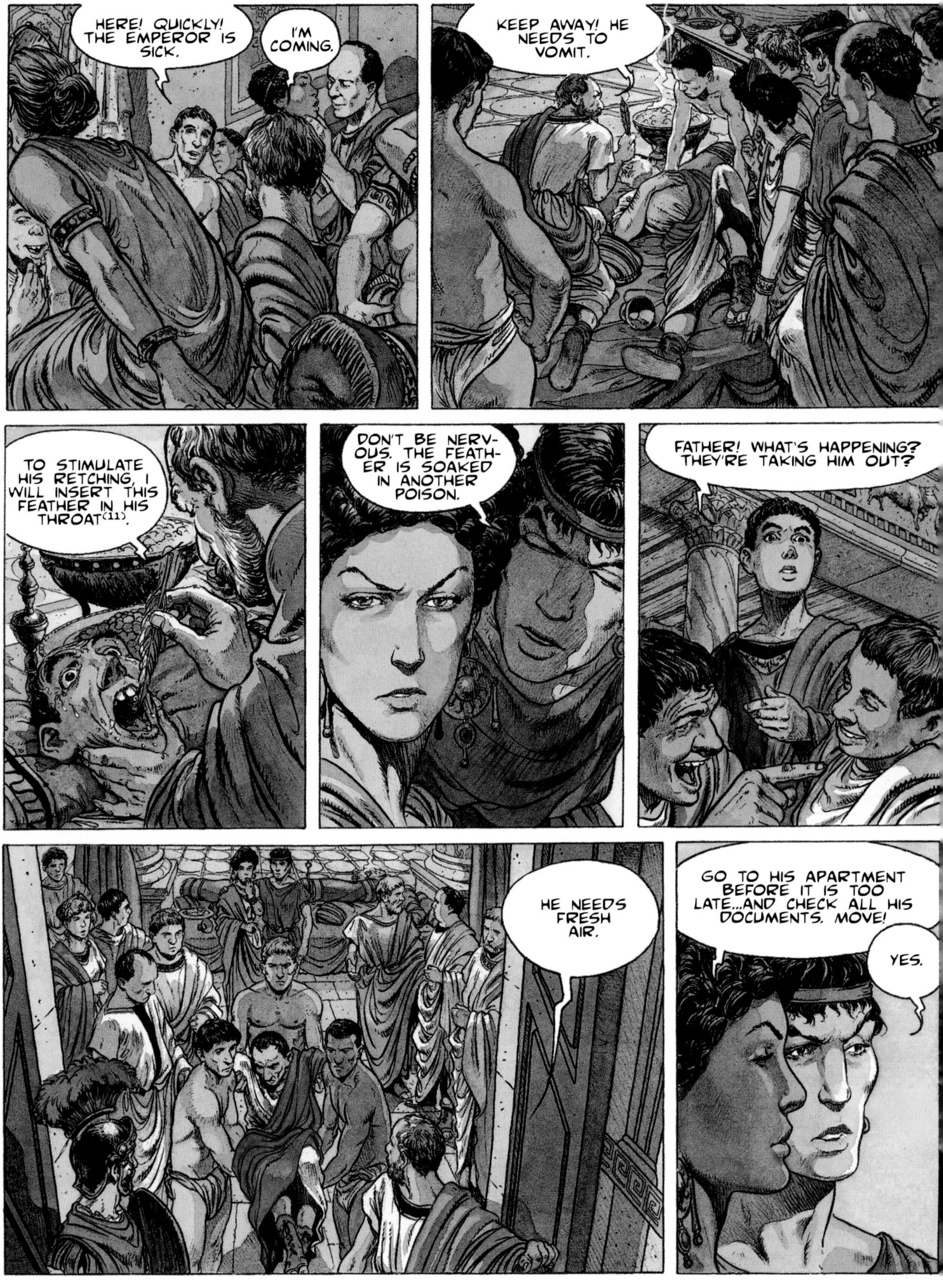
HERE! QUICKLY! THE EMPEROR IS SICK.
I'M COMING.
KEEP AWAY! HE NEEDS TO VOMIT.
TO STIMULATE HIS RETCHING, I WILL INSERT THIS FEATHER IN HIS THROAT(11).
DON'T BE NERVOUS. THE FEATHER IS SOAKED IN ANOTHER POISON.
FATHER! WHAT'S HAPPENING? THEY'RE TAKING HIM OUT?
HE NEEDS FRESH AIR.
GO TO HIS APARTMENT BEFORE IT IS TOO LATE...AND CHECK ALL HIS DOCUMENTS. MOVE!
YES.

THE EMPEROR IS SICK? IS IT SERIOUS?

THE PALACE DOORS HAVE BEEN CLOSED. THE COMMANDER OF THE PRAETORIAN GUARD IS GATHERING HIS MEN. THAT'S A BAD SIGN.

SO?

I WAS ABLE TO KEEP EVERYONE OUT. BUT HE IS CLINGING TO LIFE.

I DID WHAT I COULD.

I KNOW. YOU SHALL BE REWARDED. HE MUST DIE NOW.

HMMMM... THERE IS A WAY.

WHERE IS EVERYONE? DO NOT ABANDON ME!! IT HURTS...I AM IN PAIN...

I HEARD YOU, DEAR HUSBAND.

!!?

AND LOOK WHAT I AM BRINGING...YOUR SWEET CONSOLATION...

YOUR BELOVED WANTS A LAST KISS...

47.

THE FIFTH CAESAR DIED THAT NIGHT BY MEANS OF A GALLIC POISONER AND A GREEK DOCTOR. THE EMPEROR'S TESTAMENT WAS NEVER DIVULGED AND ITS CONTENT REMAINED UNKNOWN.

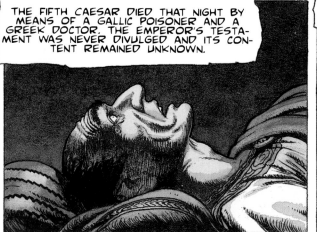

A METICULOUS SEARCH CARRIED OUT BY PALLAS IN CLAUDIUS' APARTMENT WAS PRODUCTIVE.

LOOK...AN ACT OF REJECTION...THIS MIGHT BE SOMETHING PRECIOUS TO KEEP.

CLAUDIUS' SON WAS BROUGHT TO HIS ROOM. THE SCARED BOY WAS THEN KEPT AWAY FROM THE IMPERIAL APARTMENTS, AND FROM POWER. HE WAS GRANTED NO CHANCE TO CLAIM THE THRONE, ALTHOUGH HE WOULD HAVE BEEN ENTITLED TO DO IT. THE EVIL MECHANISM STARTED BY THE EMPRESS HAD BEEN SET IN MOTION AND NOBODY COULD STOP IT!

FINALLY, BETWEEN THE SIXTH AND THE SEVENTH HOUR[12] THE DOORS OF THE PALATINE WERE OPENED TO INTRODUCE TO THE PEOPLE THE NEW EMPEROR OF ROME. THE PRAETORIAN COHORTS SOON STARTED TO LOUDLY APPLAUD HIM

NERO IS SEVENTEEN. THE MURDER COMMITTED BY HIS MOTHER PUTS HIM IN COMMAND OF THE WORLD'S GREATEST POWER. HE WAS TOLD: BE AS AMBITIOUS AS THE GODS. YOU, TOO, YOU SHALL BE A GOD...IF YOU REALLY WANT TO! SOMEBODY ELSE WANTED IT FOR HIM.

IN THIS THIRD DAY BEFORE THE IDES OF OCTOBER, THE RAIN COVERS THE CITY. ROME THE PROUD HAS JUST MET ITS NEW CAESAR. EMPEROR CLAUDIUS DIED THE PRVIOUS NIGHT. HIS SUCCESSOR IS IMPATIENT TO RISE TO POWER. HIS NAME IS LUCIUS AHENOBARBUS NERO. HE IS SEVENTEEN. IF HE SUCCEEDS IN ASSERTING HIMSELF WITH THE ARMY AND THE SENATE, HE WILL BECOME THE KING OF THE WORLD.

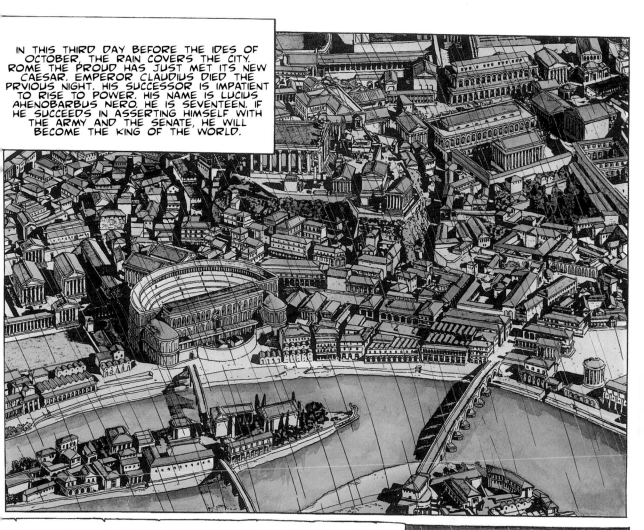

AT NOON, A LITTER FOLLOWED BY AN IMPOSING ESCORT DEPARTS FOR THE CAMP OF THE PRAETORIAN COHORTS. IT WILL CROSS THE ENTIRE CITY. THE YOUNG EMPEROR REFLECTS ABOUT WHAT IS EXPECTING HIM.

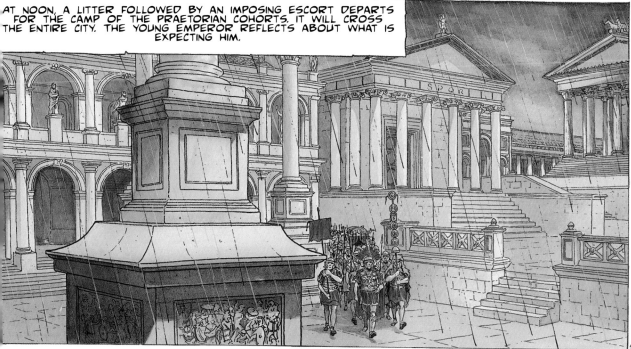

1

SIX THOUSAND MEN IN CUIRASSES, HOLDING JAVELINS AND SHIELDS PAINTED IN THE COLORS OF THE COHORT. THEIR FEET IN THE MUD, RESOLUTE FACES UNDER THEIR HELMETS.

ELITE TROOPS CREATED BY AUGUSTUS AND GATHERED IN THE CASTRA PRAETORIA, ON THE LEFT BANK OF THE TIBER RIVER. HERE IS THE FORCE OF ROME, WHICH IS ABLE TO ANOINT ONE EMPEROR AND DESTITUTE ANOTHER.

HE IS HERE!!

YOUR MEN ARE READY TO LISTEN TO YOU, CAESAR...

I...!!!

YOUR TIME HAS COME... ONE MORE STEP...JUST ONE MORE...

...AND ROME WILL BE YOURS!!

AND MY SON, HOW DID HE CONDUCT HIMSELF?

WITH ALL THE REQUIRED DIGNITY, HE PROVED TO BE RESOLUTE.

AT THE COHORTS, HE USED THE LANGUAGE THE ARMY EXPECTED TO HEAR...

FIFTEEN THOUSAND SESTERCES TO EACH PRAETORIAN. A FREE ADDITIONAL SUPPLY EVERY MONTH. THE CREATION OF A COLONY FOR VETERAN SOLDIERS IN ANTIUM...

BURRHUS HAD CLEVERLY PREPARED HIS SPEECH. NO FAULT WAS MADE. HIS WORDS WERE LARGELY PRAISED AND THE ARMY'S CONSENT WAS ABSOLUTE.

MONEY IN EXCHANGE FOR AN EMPEROR. EVERYTHING HAS ITS PRICE.

WHAT ELSE?

I TOOK CARE OF THE COURT. POOR SENATORS WILL RECEIVE REGULAR PAYMENTS UP TO 500000 SESTERCES. A LOT OF MONEY, BUT WORTH IT.

GOOD. AND THE SENATE?

SENECA TOOK CARE OF IT. YOUR SON RECEIVED A TRIUMPHAL WELCOME.

NERO WAS DECLARED SOVEREIGN MASTER OF THE EMPIRE "PRINCEPS JUVENTUTIS"[13].

NO OBSTACLE STANDS BETWEEN YOU AND THE POWER, MY MISTRESS. THE WORLD IS YOURS...

NO
STACLE.

ALL IS
REMOVED.
ONLY THE
CORE IS
LEFT...

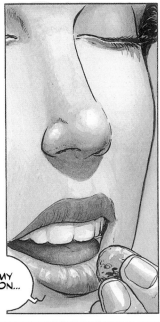

MY
SON...

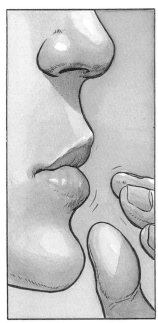

IT STOPPED
RAINING.
TONIGHT WILL
BE MILD.

THE CELEBRATIONS CAN START,
THEN. THE TRIUMPH OF OUR
NEW CAESAR WILL BE HEARD IN
THE WHOLE COURT.

YOU ARE EXPECT-
ED TO TAKE PART
IN THE CELE-
BRATIONS.

I WILL
NOT. I AM IN
MOURNING FOR
MY FATHER. THIS
WILL BE ENOUGH
TO EXCUSE MY
ABSENCE, I
THINK.

NO. IF YOU
STAY
AWAY,
SHE WILL
CRUSH
YOU,
TOO.

5.

OTHO! ARE YOU ALONE?!

BAD NEWS. I WAS AT MURENA'S HOUSE. THEY ARE IN MOURNING, HIS MOTHER WAS KILLED.

WHO? LOLIA PAULINA?

SHE DIED IN AN ATROCIOUS MANNER.

OH NO!

AGRIPPINA... HER REVENGE...

YOU LOOK PENSIVE, MY DEAR SON.

?!

LOLIA PAULINA'S DEAD MOTHER.

OH YES! I HEARD. AN ACCIDENT, COR-RECT?

6.

NOT ACCORDING TO THEM! REMEMBER HER SON IS ONE OF MY FRIENDS.

HIS MOURNING IS OURS, THEN...

...UNTIL THIS CUP IS EMPTY.

OTHON! GATHER THE OTHERS. TAKE YOUR SWORDS! NOBODY WILL STOP ME, TONIGHT.

AGREED!

LOOK WHO'S HERE! HE DARED TO LEAVE HIS HOLE!!

THE YOUNG BOY CLOSE TO THE TABLE... PUSH HIM!!

THIS JOY, THIS LAUGHTER ...NOBODY MISSES MY FATHER, THEN?

HEY!!

WATCH OUT!!

YOUNG IMBECILE! YOU STAINED MY TUNIC! LOOK!!

MY...MY APOLOGIES! I DO NOT KNOW WHAT HAPPENED. I THINK I FELL, THEN...

WE ALL SAW THAT YOU FELL! THIS IS NOT AN EXCUSE!

I DON'T KNOW WHAT KEEPS ME FROM...

LEAVE HIM ALONE!!

YOU... YOU DARE TO TOUCH ME, SLAVE?

YOU'RE A SLAVE LIKE ME. I CAN STILL SMELL THE SWEAT...

...OF THE ARENA, THE GREASE OF A GLADIATOR.

THE STAKES! RAISE THE STAKES!!

8

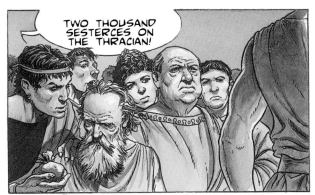

TWO THOUSAND SESTERCES ON THE THRACIAN!

I DON'T WANT TO FIGHT.

REALLY? ARE YOU AFRAID OF ME...

...SLAVE?

ONE THOUSAND ON THE BLACK! WHO WANTS TO BET?

A THOUSAND ON THE THRACIAN!! FOUR THOUSAND DRACHMAS ON THE BLACK! TO THE DEATH! TO THE DEATH!

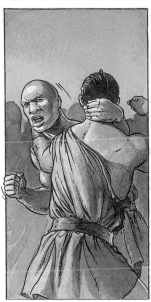

9

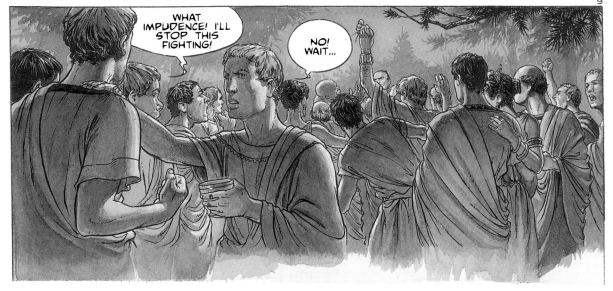

WHAT IMPUDENCE! I'LL STOP THIS FIGHTING!

NO! WAIT...

WE HAVE SOMETHING ELSE TO DO! FOLLOW ME.

THE BLACK IS WINNING!!

RAAAAH!!

10.

AAOW

THE THRACIAN WILL WIN!

THE BLACK IS HURT!

HE'S STAGGERING!!

TWO THOUSAND... ADD TWO THOUSAND DRACHMAS!!

ENOUGH! STOP THIS COMBAT!!

GUARDS, SEPARATE THEM, IF THEY DON'T!

OH! WHAT'S WITH HIM? HE NEVER ACTED THIS WAY!

SO THE SON OF CLAUDIUS, COMMANDS!

INTERESTING...

HE FOUND HIS FATHER'S VOICE...THE POWER LIES INSIDE HIM...

I WILL SEE YOU AGAIN!

I'LL BE HERE!

NERO? I THINK HE LEFT. I DO NOT KNOW WHERE HE...

MY SON...WHERE IS MY SON?

YOU UNDERSTAND MY ORDERS! NO RETREAT!!!

THIS TIME, THEY WILL LET US IN!!

I AM HERE TO SEE ACTEE.

OH YEAH?

COME BACK TOMORROW MORNING...SHE'S BUSY. SHE'S GOT SOME CUSTOMERS YOU KNOW.

SHE'S GOOD AT BUSYING HERSELF, YOUR BITCH. RIGHT, MY FRIENDS?

YOU DO UNDERSTAND, DON'T YOU? THE WORLD HAS CHANGED, TONIGHT.

YOU ARE NOTHING!!

HHHH...

TAKE THEM!!

WHAT'S GOING ON? THEY'RE FIGHTING!

!!?

COME! NO TIME TO WASTE!!

OUT OF THE WAY. MOVE!

NOT SO FAST!!!

13.

YOU WON'T ESCAPE ME, THIS TIME!!

TAKE HER!

NOTHING MUST BE LEFT OF THIS FILTHY SEWER!!

FIRE! FIRE!!!

WHAT'S WRONG? DO NOT STAY HERE!! COME!

THOSE FLAMES

"BEAUTIFUL...I HAVE NEVER SEEN ANYTHING SO BEAUTIFUL..."

A RED GLOW IS RISING...

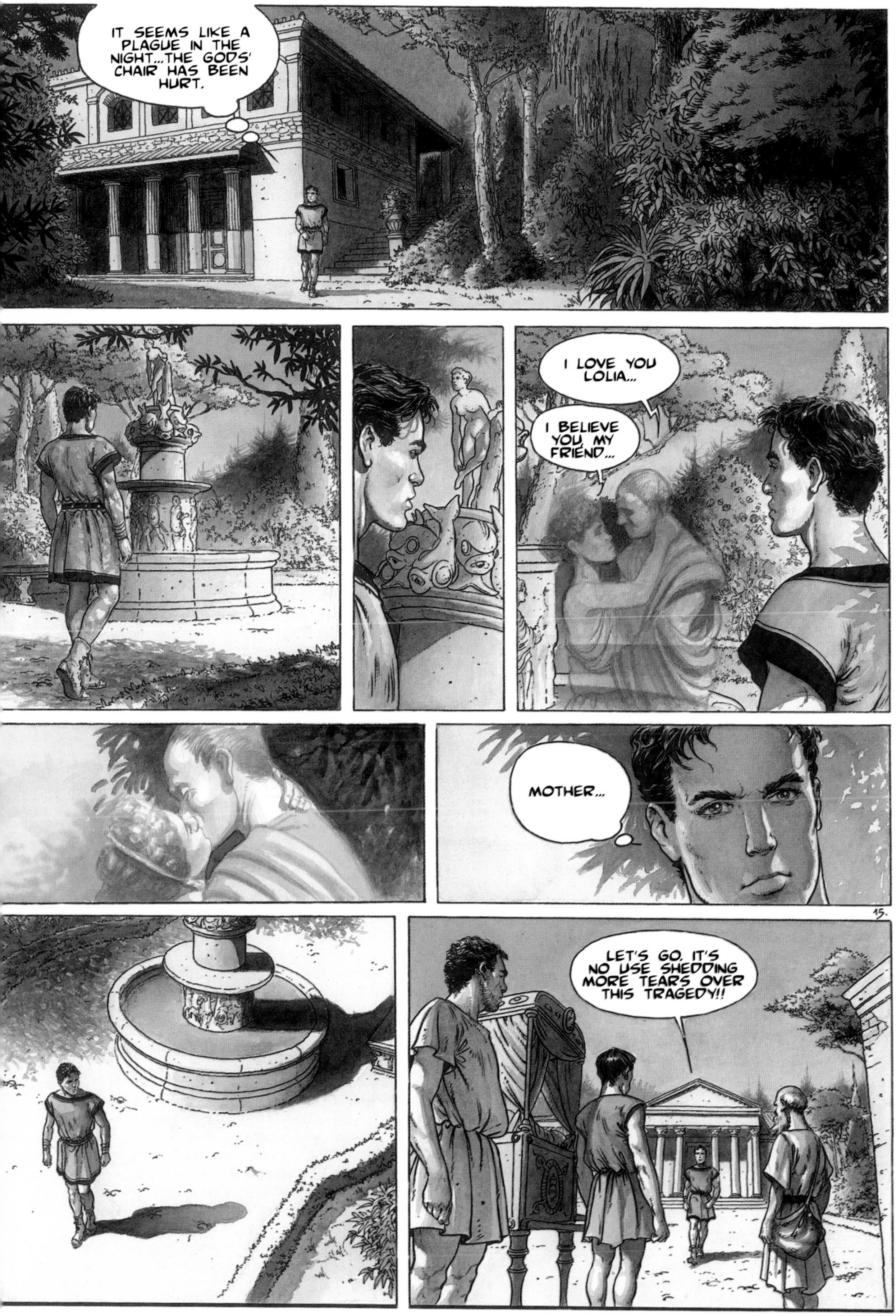
IT SEEMS LIKE A PLAGUE IN THE NIGHT...THE GODS' CHAIR HAS BEEN HURT.
I LOVE YOU LOLIA...
I BELIEVE YOU, MY FRIEND...
MOTHER...
15.
LET'S GO, IT'S NO USE SHEDDING MORE TEARS OVER THIS TRAGEDY!!

DID YOU PUT OUT THE SACRED FIRE?

YES. NOTHING NEEDS OUR PROTECTION HERE[14].

WHERE NOW?

TO THE HOUSE OF A FRIEND WHO WILL HOST US, PETRONIUS ARBITER[5].

THERE IS A NEW FIRE BURNING OVER ROME...HAVE YOU SEEN IT?

OMEN OF EVIL!!

YOU SAVED MY LIFE.

YOU'RE JOKING? YOU COULD'VE BEATEN HIM.

NO. THE THRACIAN SLAVE IS STRONGER.

THE HATRED IS STILL IN HIM, I LOST MINE.

YOU COULD MAKE A LOT OF MONEY HAVING ME FIGHT.

HOW?

I CAN BECOME A FIGHTER NOBODY CAN BEAT. YOU'LL GET RICH. IT'S MONEY YOU NEED.

BUT WHY?

16

"TO REGAIN YOUR THRONE FROM THE USURPER EMPRESS..."

I...I CANNOT ACCEPT SUCH BARBAROUS ACTS! THE GIRL IS MINE, I INVESTED AN ENORMOUS AMOUNT OF MONEY ON HER...I WANT HER BACK! BEFORE THAT...THAT... THAT SAVAGE RUINS HER.

WAIT! IS IT MY SON THAT YOU ARE CALLING SAVAGE?

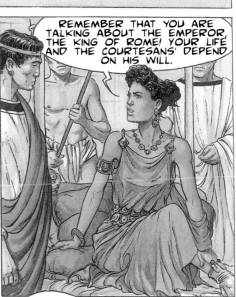

REMEMBER THAT YOU ARE TALKING ABOUT THE EMPEROR, THE KING OF ROME! YOUR LIFE AND THE COURTESANS' DEPEND ON HIS WILL.

YOU SHOULD FEEL LUCKY FOR THE ESTEEM YOU HAVE ALWAYS BEEN HELD IN! STOP BOTHERING US WITH YOUR VULGAR TRAFICINGS. NOW, GET OUT OF HERE, I HAVE HEARD ENOUGH!

WHAT ?

OH! SHE WILL PAY FOR THIS AFFRONT!!!

YOUR SLAVE CANNOT RESTRAIN HIMSELF.

I DON'T CARE! HE'S REVEALING HIS TRUE NATURE, I NEED TO TAKE CARE OF HIM.

17

LEAVE US!

ANY NEWS, MY FRIEND?

YOUR SON IS AT HIS AUNT'S HOUSE. HE IS NOT ALONE, APPARENTLY. A SLAVE IS WITH HIM.

HMM...IT'S ACTEE. HE TOLD ME ABOUT HER. AND HE STOLE HER FROM PALLAS' CONTROL. COULD HE BE...

...IN LOVE WITH HER? THEY ARE THE SAME AGE.

HE'S NOT BEEN APPEASED BY HIS MARRIAGE[16].

NO DOUBT. BUT THAT'S NOT THE REASON.

HE WAS FORBIDDEN TO SEE DOMITIA! GO THERE AND BRING HIM BACK, QUICKLY!

YES, MISTRESS. AND THE SLAVE?

"I HEARD SHE IS VERY BEAUTIFUL."

ACTEE?

MY SERVANTS ARE PREPARING HER AS YOU REQUESTED.

18

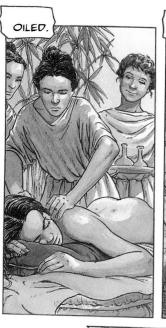

OILED.

SHAVED.

MAKE UP. HAIR STYLED.

DRESSED.

AND THEN? WHAT WILL YOU DO WITH HER?

TREAT HER LIKE A SLAVE...OR A QUEEN.

I DON'T KNOW YET.

"I WILL TALK TO HER FIRST."

I...I BROUGHT YOU THESE JEWELS.

I WOULD LIKE YOU TO WEAR THEM.

DO I HAVE A CHOICE?

WELL, THESE EARRINGS ARE YOURS. DO YOU DESIRE ANYTHING ELSE?

I WANT TO LEAVE AND NOT LOOK BACK.

AND GO BACK TO PALLAS?

PALLAS MEANS NOTHING TO ME. HE BOUGHT ME WHEN I WAS YOUNG. HE TAKES ADVANTAGE OF MY WOMAN'S BODY. AS WILL YOU, I SUPPOSE.

I SHALL LEAVE YOU THE SEC- OND EARRING. YOU WILL PUT IT ON YOURSELF.

I COULDN'T SLEEP LAST NIGHT. I'M TIRED. MY SLAVES WILL SHOW YOU MY ROOM, IF YOU WISH TO JOIN ME.

OTHERWISE ...YOU CAN LEAVE, YOU ARE FREE.

!?

AAH!

MY REGARDS, DOMITIA LEPIDA. I CAME TO SEE THE YOUNG EMPEROR.

HE'S RESTING. BUT I'LL INFORM HIM YOU'RE HERE.

WELL, LET HIM SLEEP. I THINK HE DESERVES IT. I WAS TOLD ABOUT YOUR DELICIOUS HONEY CAKES, DOMITIA.

OH, YES. PLEASE, HAVE SOME. YOU WILL NOT BE DISAPPOINTED.

TELL ME SOMETHING ABOUT THIS YOUNG SLAVE.

HE LIKES HER, HE CANNOT HIDE IT...

20.

MMM?

YOU? YOU...YOU'VE BEEN THERE A LONG TIME?

I WAS LOOKING AT YOU, AND I HAVE SEEN WHAT I WANTED TO SEE.

YOU SLEPT ENOUGH, I THINK. LET ME IN.

ACTEE...

EVERY TIME THE SAME...A DOUBLE THREAT...THE FACE OF A YOUNG BOY, THE FACE OF A WOMAN...WE NEED TO ACT QUICKLY, THE LIVER IS ABOUT TO BURST.

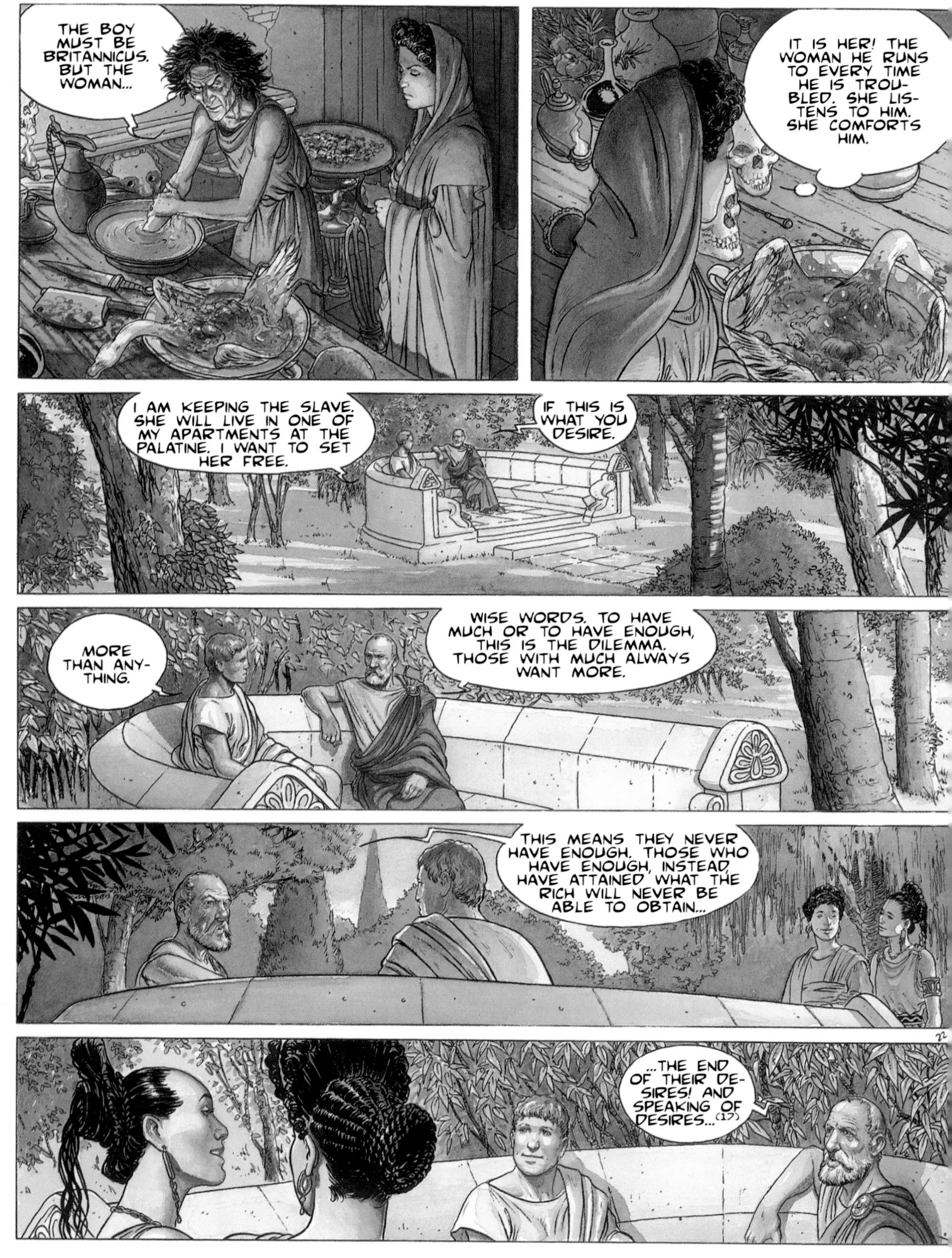
THE BOY MUST BE BRITANNICUS. BUT THE WOMAN...
IT IS HER! THE WOMAN HE RUNS TO EVERY TIME HE IS TROUBLED. SHE LISTENS TO HIM. SHE COMFORTS HIM.
I AM KEEPING THE SLAVE. SHE WILL LIVE IN ONE OF MY APARTMENTS AT THE PALATINE. I WANT TO SET HER FREE.
IF THIS IS WHAT YOU DESIRE.
MORE THAN ANYTHING.
WISE WORDS. TO HAVE MUCH OR TO HAVE ENOUGH, THIS IS THE DILEMMA. THOSE WITH MUCH ALWAYS WANT MORE.
THIS MEANS THEY NEVER HAVE ENOUGH. THOSE WHO HAVE ENOUGH, INSTEAD, HAVE ATTAINED WHAT THE RICH WILL NEVER BE ABLE TO OBTAIN...
...THE END OF THEIR DESIRES! AND SPEAKING OF DESIRES...(17)
22

YOU ARE LEAVING.

I MUST. BUT THIS TIME, I WILL NOT BE ALONE. SHE WILL BE WITH ME.

TAKE CARE OF YOURSELF. AND HOLD OUT...

HOLD OUT AGAINST WHAT, MY DEAR DOMITIA?

YOURSELF MY CHILD, YOURSELF.

THE FOLLOWING DAY, AT DAWN. BACCHUS SOROCTOS' SCHOOL FOR GLADIATORS...

HOLA! IS ANYONE HERE??

WHAT DO YOU WANT? GET OUT OF HERE!

I AM LOOKING FOR BACCHUS SOROCTOS.

REALLY?! WELL, YOU KNOW, HE'S NOT LOOKING FOR ANYONE.

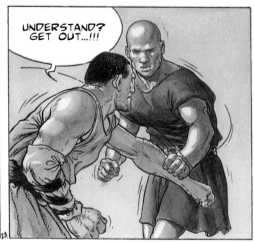

UNDERSTAND? GET OUT...!!!

AAAAHH!!

YOU DIRTY...!!!

MMPFF...

AARGNN!!

GRR..AHC!

BRAVO! YOU CAN DEFEND YOURSELF.

AND YOU ALSO COST ME A LOT OF MONEY!!

IT'S...IT'S HIS FAULT IF...

IDIOT! SHUT UP OR I'LL BREAK YOUR ARM!

AND THIS ONE IS NOW USELESS. A REAL PITY! HE WAS STARTING TO MAKE MONEY.

YOU ARE BACCHUS SOROCTOS...?

AT YOUR SERVICE...WITHIN THE LIMITS OF MY ABILITIES, OF COURSE.

I WANT TO LEARN HOW TO FIGHT, HOW TO WIN.

REALLY? I THINK YOU'RE ALREADY WELL TRAINED FOR THAT.

THIS IS TRUE. I KNOW THE ARENA. I FOUGHT THERE MANY TIMES AND I SURVIVED. BUT THAT WILL NOT LAST. I NEED TO LEARN WHAT COUNTS MOST.

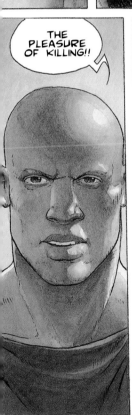

THE PLEASURE OF KILLING!!

KILLING AND NOT BEING KILLED IS MY TRADE. BUT THIS WILL COST YOU A LOT OF MONEY

I CAN PAY!!

IN THAT CASE, I'M SURE WE CAN REACH AN AGREEMENT. FOLLOW ME. I'LL DRAW A CONTRACT THAT'LL SATISFY BOTH.

RRRAHHHHH

??

STOP!
MERCY! MERCY!

DO YOU HEAR THAT? HE'S HAD ENOUGH.

I SAID ALL, YOU GOT IT? ALL. AND SATIS-FY THEM AS YOU SATISFIED ME!

HEY! STOP IT!

WHAT ARE YOU STARING AT? AH...YES. THEY ARE SLAVES. I FOUND THEM THE SILESIA MINES. REAL BEASTS. THEIR "EDUCATION" IS SLOWER...BUT...

"...ONCE TAMED THEY'LL BECOME POWERFUL FIGHTERS. THERE IS ONE, IN PARTICULAR..."

"...MASSAM. HE ALREADY KILLED TWO OF MY TRAINERS. BUT I MADE MORE MONEY FROM HIM THAN ANYONE ELSE."

HEY! STRANGER! COME HERE. I'VE NEVER TASTED BLACK MEAT. COME. I PROMISE YOU'LL HAVE FUN.

26.

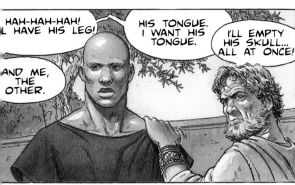

HAH-HAH-HAH! I HAVE HIS LEG!

HIS TONGUE. I WANT HIS TONGUE.

I'LL EMPTY HIS SKULL... ALL AT ONCE!

AND ME, THE OTHER.

CAREFUL! THEY ARE BLOOD-THIRSTY!!

SO I SEE!

THEY'RE ORGANIZING A GREAT BANQUET. TRIMACHION IS A GOOD HOST.

DO YOU REALLY THINK I'M IN THE MOOD FOR THE CLAMOR OF A CROWD?

THIS FAKE ENJOYMENT, ALL THE CHATTERING.

THE CHATTERING WE NEED, THOUGH.

YOU WON'T FIND YOUR MOTHER'S MURDERERS BY SHUTTING YOURSELF UP IN YOUR HOUSE. YOU NEED TO CIRCULATE...MINGLE WITH THE CROWD AND YOU'LL GET TO THE TRUTH.

AH! OUR MAN IS APPROACHING! FOLLOW ME, I WANT YOU TO MEET HIM. DO YOU STILL TRUST ME?

YES, YOU KNOW I DO.

27.

THEN, MARCUS BRUTUS CAN BE OF GREAT HELP.

I HAVE SOME NEWS.

AH! JUST WHAT I EXPECTED FROM YOU!!

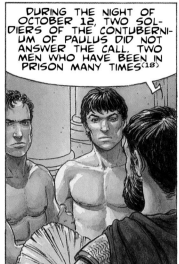

DURING THE NIGHT OF OCTOBER 12, TWO SOLDIERS OF THE CONTUBERNIUM OF PAULUS DID NOT ANSWER THE CALL, TWO MEN WHO HAVE BEEN IN PRISON MANY TIMES (18)

WE FOUND THEM AT DAWN, DRUNK, IN A TAVERN NOT FAR FROM WHERE THE CRIME WAS COMMITTED. I ASKED TO SEE THEM. I QUESTIONED THEM SEPARATELY.

AND?

HERE IS WHERE THE STORY GETS INTERESTING. THEY BOTH REPORTED TWO SIMILAR PLANS FOR THAT NIGHT. TOO SIMILAR, I WOULD SAY. THE DETAILS ALMOST ENTIRELY CORRESPONDED...THE PROBLEM, I DID NOT ASK FOR SO MANY DETAILS...

THEY WERE RELEASED?

ONE WAS. I WANT TO PRESSURE THE SECOND ONE. IF HE TALKS, I'LL LET YOU KNOW.

THIS IS NOT THE FIRST TIME ONE OF OUR MEN DID THIS SORT OF THING.

WHAT MAN WOULD NOT DO FOR MONEY, RIGHT, MARCUS BRUTUS?

I DIDN'T KNOW YOU MIXED WITH THAT KIND OF PEOPLE

WELL, HE'S NOT BAD. HE NEGLECTS HIS WIFE, HE HITS HIS CHILDREN, HE'D SELL HIS MOTHER, BUT HIS CONSCIENCE LETS HIM LIVE. THAT'S WHAT COUNTS, RIGHT?

PETRONIUS...

YES?

HOW CAN I THANK YOU?

BY LISTENING TO SOME OF MY VERSES. A HIGH COST, I KNOW.

A FEW WEEKS HAVE PASSED. BUT WHAT IS TIME TO THE GODS? A BREATH, THE SHADOW OF A GRAIN ON THE GROUND, A FURTIVE DESIRE GLIDING ALONG AN ILLUSION. NOTHING FOR WHICH IS WORTH OPENING THEIR EYES.

YOU. IT IS YOU WHO ARRANGED THIS ENCOUNTER?!!

YOU DID NOT EXPECT PALLAS? DON'T WORRY. NOBODY EXPECTS PALLAS ANYMORE

I HAVE A DOCUMENT I FOUND IN YOUR FATHER'S APARTMENTS, WHEN HE DIED. ANOTHER WAY OF INTERPRETING HISTORY.

I DON'T UNDER-STAND.

THAT'S NORMAL. YOU NEVER WERE SUPPOSED TO UNDERSTAND. EVEN MY MISTRESS IS UNAWARE OF THIS DOCUMENT.

YOU'RE TALKING ABOUT MY STEP-MOTHER.

ARE YOU READY TO BETRAY HER, TOO?

SHE DOESN'T LISTEN TO ME, NOW. I AM LOOKING FOR ANOTHER LIS-TENER WHO CAN APPRECIATE THE VALUE OF MY WORDS.

LIKE THIS DOCUMENT[19]...AN ACT OF REJECTION WITH YOUR FATHER'S SEAL. IT OFFICIALLY PREVENTS YOUR STEPBROTHER FROM CLAIMING ANY RIGHT OF SUCCESSION.

YOUR FATHER WROTE IT BEFORE HE DIED. HE REJECTED NERO. YOU ARE HIS SUCCESSOR.

IT IS IMPRESSIVE. BUT WHO WILL SUPPORT ME, IF I DECIDE TO CLAIM THE AUTHENTICITY OF THIS TESTAMENT? I WILL BE ALONE AGAINST THE EMPRESS.

YOU HAVE NO CHOICE, MY FRIEND...

IT IS HER, OR YOU! AND TO PROVE THIS, I WANT YOU TO COME TONIGHT ON THE BANK OF MULVIUS BRIDGE, AT THE EXIT OF THE VIA FLAMINIA.

MULVIUS BRIDGE, THE PLACE WHERE NERO HAS HIS NIGHT ESCAPADES. I'D RATHER NOT SEE HIM.

NERO DOESN'T LEAVE HIS APARTMENTS FOR LONG. HE'S IN LOVE, NOW...

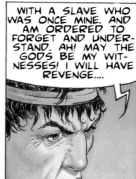

WITH A SLAVE WHO WAS ONCE MINE. AND AM ORDERED TO FORGET AND UNDERSTAND. AH! MAY THE GODS BE MY WITNESSES! I WILL HAVE REVENGE....

WAIT! DID YOU HEAR SOMETHING?

IT WAS LIKE MUTTERING...

NO... NOBODY IS HERE.

I MUST HAVE DREAMT...

HE NEVER LEAVES HER.

ACTEE. YES. SHE IS BEAUTIFUL, ISN'T SHE?

HE SEEMS DEEPLY IN LOVE WITH HER.

ND THIS IS BETTER FOR ME. A HEART IN LOVE OES NOT WORRY ABOUT POWER. I SHALL CONTINUE GOVERNING BY MYSELF!

I'LL BE BUSY TONIGHT. IF ANYBODY LOOKS FOR ME, THROW HIM TO THE LIONS.

WHAT?

RELAX, I WAS JUST TEASING YOU.

WHEW! WITH THIS WITCH, YOU NEVER KNOW!

HE IS ONE OF MY DEAREST FRIENDS. PLEASE, WELCOME HIM WITH COURTESY.

HE SUFFERED, YOU SAID?

YES. HE HAS JUST LOST HIS MOTHER. HERE HE COMES!

IS THAT YOUNG MURENA? THE SON OF LOLIA PAULINA?

HE IS. HE INHERITED A FORTUNE FROM HIS MOTHER.

LISTEN! YOU WANTED TO TALK, BUT YOU HAVEN'T SAID A WORD ABOUT THE CHARMING WOMAN WITH ME, ARE YOU BLIND TO HER BEAUTY?

ONE NIGHT YOU SAW HER FROM AFAR. YOU SAID SHE WAS FASCINATING.

ACTEE! OF COURSE.

NOW I WHY YOU SO RADIANT, LOVED BEST MEN.

UNDERSTAND ARE SO YOU ARE BY THE OF ALL

LET ME OFFER YOU THIS PRESENT. THIS JEWEL BELONGED TO MY MOTHER, IN A HAPPY TIME, WHEN I USED TO HEAR HER LAUGHING.

THANK YOU MY FRIEND. I WILL NOT FORGET THIS.

WE LOVE YOU, TOO.

HMM...EITHER THE FRIEND IS HEARTFELT OR THE COURTESAN IS CUNNING.

YOU LOOK SO NERVOUS. WHAT DO YOU WANT TO TELL ME?

IT IS ABOUT LOLIA PAULINA. I THINK I FOUND HER MURDERERS.

WH...WHAT??

I DIDN'T WANT TO BELIEVE IT, BUT AMONG THE MEN IN OUR HOUSE THAT NIGHT, THERE WERE SOME SOLDIERS OF THE GUARD!

OF MY GUARD?? ARE...ARE YOU SURE?

ONE OF THEM WAS ARRESTED AND CONFESSED HIS DEED.

DID HE WORK ALONE?

NO. AN OLD GLADIATOR MET HIM IN A TAVERN AND PAID HIM TO KILL MY MOTHER. A MAN WHO SEEMS TO HAVE ACCESS TO THE IMPERIAL PALACE.

DRAXIUS! MY MOTHER'S SLAVE!!!

WHO...WHO TOLD YOU ABOUT THIS SOLDIER?

A CENTURION NAMED MARCUS BRUTUS. HELP ROMISED TO HELP ME. I WILL REWARD HIM, OF COURSE.

GOOD. I WILL TAKE CARE OF THIS AFFAIR.

33.

BE CAREFUL! THE STEPS ARE SLIPPERY!

WHAT A SMELL! WHY DID YOU PUT THIS MAN DOWN HERE?

THESE ARE THE ORDERS OF MARCUS BRUTUS. I KNOW NO MORE.

WILL IT TAKE LONG?

IT WILL ALL DEPEND ON HIS ANSWERS.

STAND UP! YOU HAVE GUESTS.

!!?

TELL ME, ARE YOU ONE OF THE GUYS WHO ARE SUSPECTED OF PARTICIPATING IN LOLIA PAULINA'S MURDER?

I...I WAS NOT ALONE! I...I JUST OBEYED...

I WILL CARRY THE TORCH. YOU CAN LEAVE.

REST ASSURED, YOU WON'T HAVE TO OBEY ANYONE AGAIN!

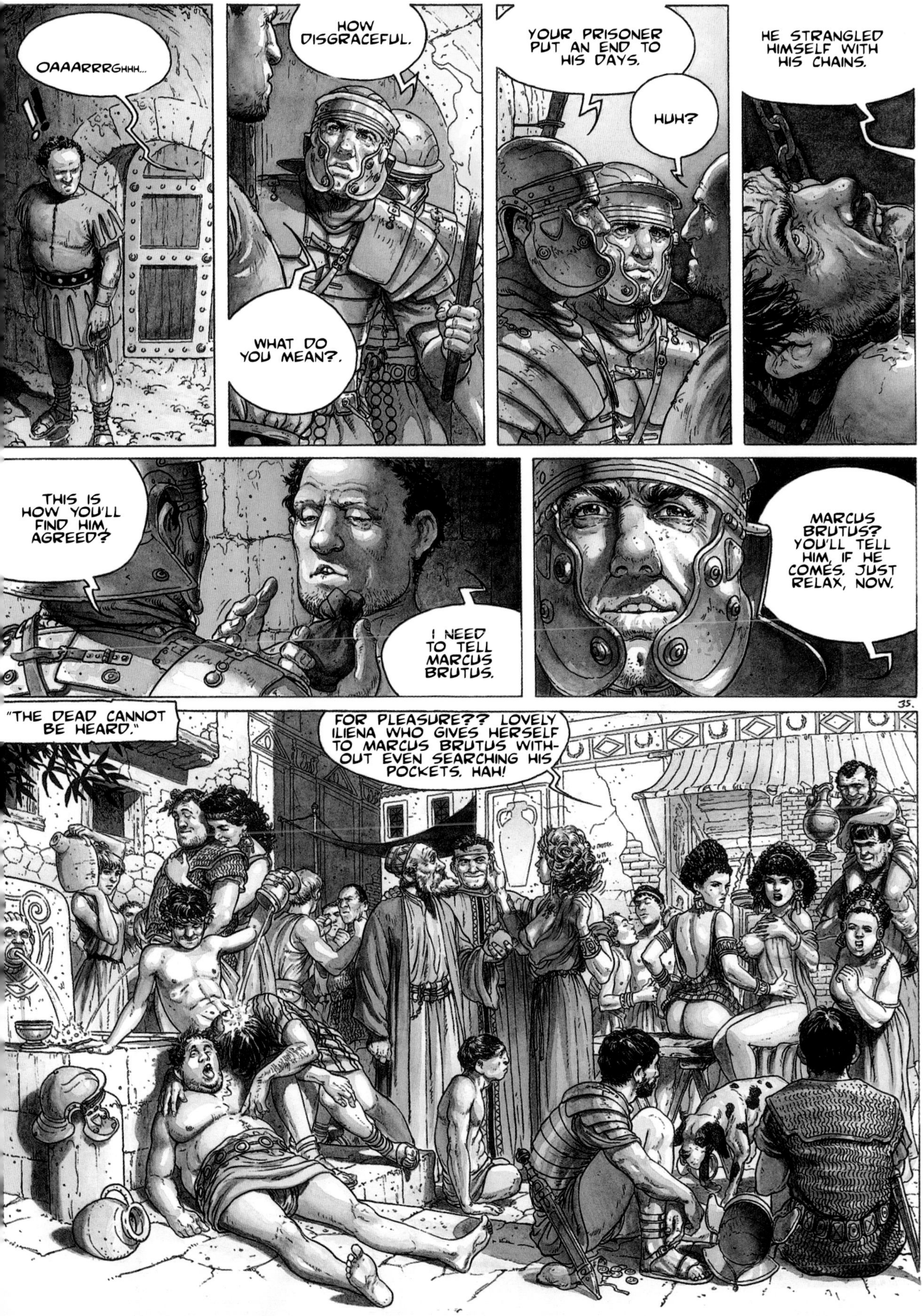

OAAARRRGHHH...
!!
HOW DISGRACEFUL.
WHAT DO YOU MEAN?.
YOUR PRISONER PUT AN END TO HIS DAYS.
HUH?
HE STRANGLED HIMSELF WITH HIS CHAINS.
THIS IS HOW YOU'LL FIND HIM, AGREED?
I NEED TO TELL MARCUS BRUTUS.
MARCUS BRUTUS? YOU'LL TELL HIM, IF HE COMES. JUST RELAX, NOW.
"THE DEAD CANNOT BE HEARD."
FOR PLEASURE?? LOVELY ILIENA WHO GIVES HERSELF TO MARCUS BRUTUS WITHOUT EVEN SEARCHING HIS POCKETS. HAH!

STOP, MARCUS! YOU'RE DRUNK. YOU'LL LOSE YOUR STRENGTH

WHY DON'T WE HAVE SOME FUN? THERE'S A FREE ROOM AT THE END OF THE CORRIDOR.

WHY DIDN'T YOU TELL ME SOONER? COME! YOU NEED TO SEE HOW STRONG I AM.

THE LAST ROOM, YOU SAID.

WE'RE ALONE, HERE, ALL THE BEDROOMS ARE EMPTY!

IT'S HIM!

HELP ME!!

I'M BEING KILLED!!

IT'S OVER. YOU KNOW WHAT FOLLOWS?

YES, YES. MARCUS WAS ROBBED... AND...AND I OWE MY LIFE TO MY QUICK ESCAPE.

WHO TALKED ABOUT ESCAPE?

MURDER! MURDER!

RUN!

OUCH!!!

BY JUPITER! THOSE PEOPLE ARE CERTAINLY IN A HURRY.

HOW STRANGE! I THINK I RECOGNIZED ONE OF THE EMPEROR'S SLAVES.

COME! WE HAVE WASTED ENOUGH TIME.

YES, YOU'RE RIGHT.

IT'S HERE! I KNOW THIS PLACE!

SO, YOU KNOW WHO LIVES HERE?

NO, I...I NEVER DARED TO ENTER, BUT I'VE SEEN THIS HOUSE IN ONE OF MY DREAMS, A REAL NIGHTMARE!

A NIGHTMARE?

GOOD CHOICE OF WORDS. FOLLOW ME.

QUIET... SHE JUST ARRIVED!

PERFECT! YOU KNOW WHAT I NEED.

YES, YOUR FRIEND WANTS TO SEE IT WITH HIS OWN EYES.

EVERY THING'S READY. THE DOOR'S NOT A PROBLEM NOW.

MAKE NO NOISE, THEIR ROOM IS RIGHT NEXT TO OURS!

CAREFUL. THE FLOOR IS WET.

YOU CAN SEE EVERYTHING.

OH! BY THE GODS! IT'S HER!!!

SO?

THE HEART IS STILL BEATING...I SHAL EX-TRACT ITS FLUID AND SEND IT TO THE PALACE.

YOU WILL SEE. NO LOVE POTION IS AS STRONG AS THIS ONE.

PERFECT!

I NEED TO KNOW WHO IT IS FOR.

MY SON. HE IS INFATUATED WITH A SLAVE, VERY BEAUTI-FUL, I MUST SAY. THEY SPEND A LOT OF TIME TOGETHER.

39

I WANT HIM TO THINK ABOUT HER ALL THE TIME.

I UNDERSTAND... YOU WILL HAVE FULL POWER OVER THE EMPIRE.

IT IS CONVENIENT FOR ME, TOO. BUT, YOU NEVER THOUGHT ABOUT THE OTHER...THE SON OF THE LATE EMPEROR.

BRITANNICUS? BAH, WHAT WORKED FOR CLAUDIUS WILL WORK FOR HIS SON.

DO YOU HAVE SOME OF THAT POISON LEFT?

ENOUGH FOR THE SON TO JOIN HIS FATHER.

I...I FEEL SICK. OH! I'M SUFFOCATING.

QUICK! THEY'RE LEAVING!!!

IT'S AGREED, THEN? IN THREE DAYS.

I'LL BE READY.

FEELING BETTER?

I SUFFER FROM THE GOD'S DISEASE[20]. I...I THINK I WAS ABOUT TO HAVE AN ATTACK.

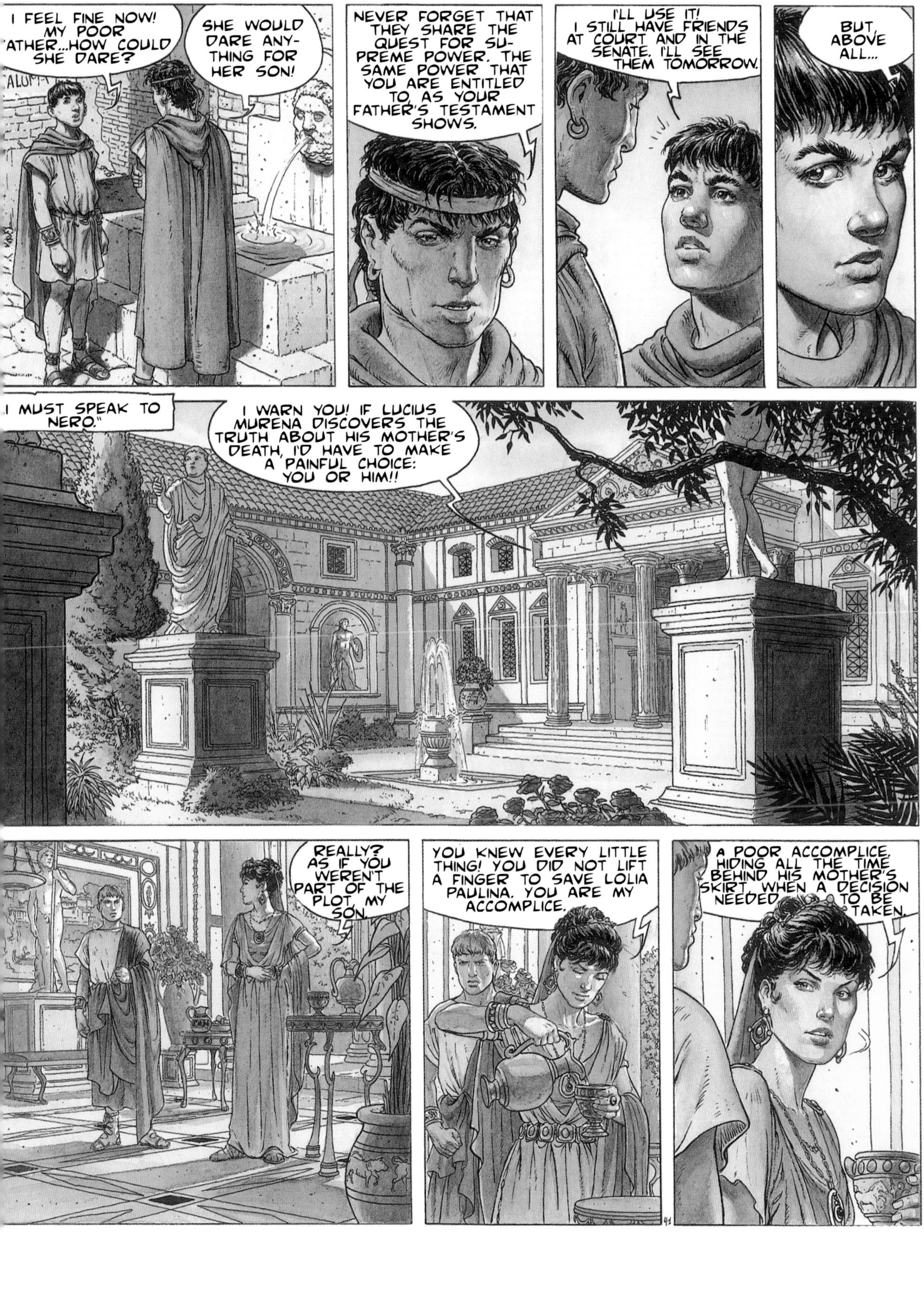

I FEEL FINE NOW! MY POOR FATHER...HOW COULD SHE DARE?
SHE WOULD DARE ANYTHING FOR HER SON!
NEVER FORGET THAT THEY SHARE THE QUEST FOR SUPREME POWER. THE SAME POWER THAT YOU ARE ENTITLED TO, AS YOUR FATHER'S TESTAMENT SHOWS.
I'LL USE IT! I STILL HAVE FRIENDS AT COURT AND IN THE SENATE. I'LL SEE THEM TOMORROW.
BUT, ABOVE ALL...
I MUST SPEAK TO NERO."
I WARN YOU! IF LUCIUS MURENA DISCOVERS THE TRUTH ABOUT HIS MOTHER'S DEATH, I'D HAVE TO MAKE A PAINFUL CHOICE: YOU OR HIM!!
REALLY? AS IF YOU WEREN'T PART OF THE PLOT, MY SON.
YOU KNEW EVERY LITTLE THING! YOU DID NOT LIFT A FINGER TO SAVE LOLIA PAULINA. YOU ARE MY ACCOMPLICE.
A POOR ACCOMPLICE, HIDING ALL THE TIME BEHIND HIS MOTHER'S SKIRT WHEN A DECISION NEEDED TO BE TAKEN.

ENOUGH! I SHALL NOT TOLERATE THAT!!

I WARN YOU...I WILL NEVER BE YOUR ACCOMPLICE AGAIN! NOW, I AM IN POWER! THE ONLY ONE IN POWER! AND I WILL NOT LET ANYONE INTERFERE WITH MY WILL, IS IT CLEAR?

NOT EVEN YOU...THE BEST OF ALL MOTHERS!

WELL, WELL...

I HAVE NEVER SEEN THAT EXPRESSION ON HER FACE. ONE WOULD SAY SHE IS SCARED.

HE WILL CHANGE HIS MIND. HE RESISTS ME NOW, BUT EVERY SON RETURNS TO HIS MOTHER.

I'M LISTENING.

WE ACTED QUICKLY, AS YOU REQUESTED. NEITHER MARCUS BRUTUS NOR THE PRISONER WILL EVER TALK AGAIN.

PERFECT. I JUST NEED A JUSTIFICATION FOR THEIR DEATHS. SOMEONE...

BURRHUS...

YES?

42

IT IS TIME FOR YOU TO CHOOSE YOUR CAMP. ARE YOU WITH ME OR WITH MY MOTHER?

I...

WITH YOU, CAESAR. I WILL OBEY YOUR ORDERS.

DURING THE NIGHT, WHEN THE ROMANS ARE CELEBRATING THE SIGILLARIA[21], BRITANNICUS IS SITTING NEAR NERO'S TABLE. AS IS THE CUSTOM, A SLAVE TASTES THE FOOD AND DRINKS OF HIS MASTER BEFORE THE MASTER CAN EAT. THE IMPERIAL FEAST HAS NOT YET TURNED INTO AN ORGY. WHEN EVERYBODY TOASTS THE NEW CAESAR, BRITAN-NICUS DOES NOT PARTICIPATE. HE IS CARRYING A PARCHMENT THAT CAN CHANGE THE DESTINY OF THE WORLD.

TO THE KING OF ROME!!!

TO CAESAR!!!

TO CAESAR!!!

AND YOU, BRITANNICUS? YOU DO NOT RAISE YOUR CUP IN MY HONOR?

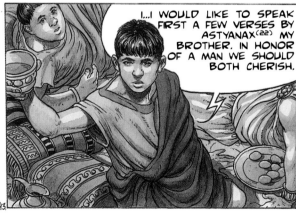

I...I WOULD LIKE TO SPEAK FIRST A FEW VERSES BY ASTYANAX[22] MY BROTHER. IN HONOR OF A MAN WE SHOULD BOTH CHERISH.

43.

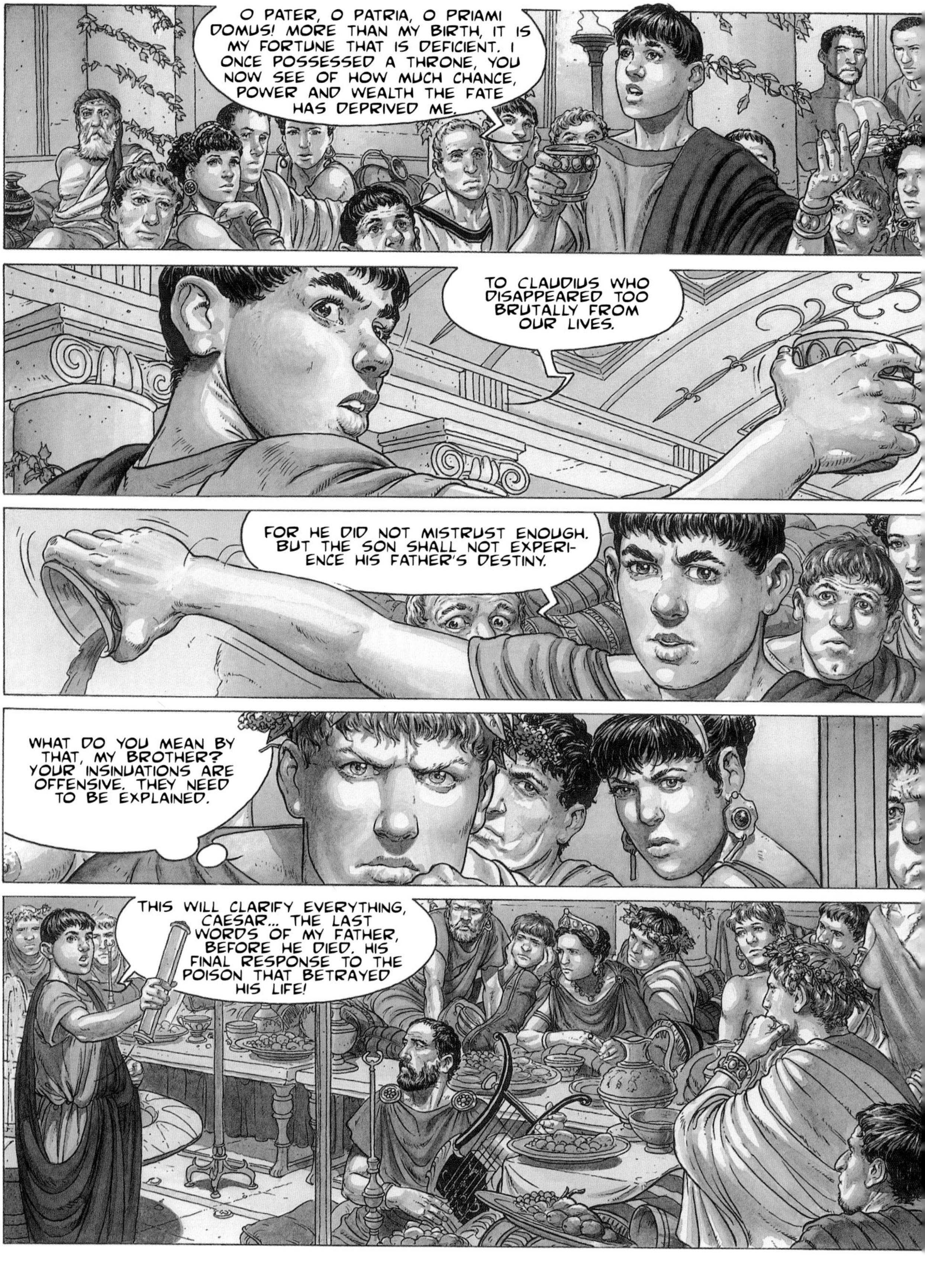
O PATER, O PATRIA, O PRIAMI DOMUS! MORE THAN MY BIRTH, IT IS MY FORTUNE THAT IS DEFICIENT. I ONCE POSSESSED A THRONE, YOU NOW SEE OF HOW MUCH CHANCE, POWER AND WEALTH THE FATE HAS DEPRIVED ME.
TO CLAUDIUS WHO DISAPPEARED TOO BRUTALLY FROM OUR LIVES.
FOR HE DID NOT MISTRUST ENOUGH. BUT THE SON SHALL NOT EXPERIENCE HIS FATHER'S DESTINY.
WHAT DO YOU MEAN BY THAT, MY BROTHER? YOUR INSINUATIONS ARE OFFENSIVE. THEY NEED TO BE EXPLAINED.
THIS WILL CLARIFY EVERYTHING, CAESAR... THE LAST WORDS OF MY FATHER, BEFORE HE DIED. HIS FINAL RESPONSE TO THE POISON THAT BETRAYED HIS LIFE!

EXCEL-
LENT!!

POISON??

WH...WHAT?
THIS CANNOT
BE TRUE!!!

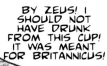

BY ZEUS! I
SHOULD NOT
HAVE DRUNK
FROM THIS CUP!
IT WAS MEANT
FOR BRITANNICUS!

THE LOVE OF A FATHER
FOR HIS ONLY CHILD! THIS
IS WHAT THIS DOCUMENT
CONTAINS!
IT DECLARES...

45.

...THAT THE ONLY
HEIR OF CLAUDIUS
IS NOBODY ELSE
BUT...BUT...

THE...THE GORGON...

AAAAHHHH! FATHER!!!!

POISON! THIS CUP WAS FULL OF POISON!!

HE...HE'S DEAD!!!

THE TESTAMENT!!!

GOT IT!!!

WAIT!!

THE DOCUMENT...I WANT TO BE THE FIRST ONE TO READ IT.

THIS IS AN ORDER. WHAT ARE YOU WAITING FOR?

FACING THE EMPIRE... THE WHOLE EMPIRE BY MYSELF.

HERE IT IS, CAESAR. I COLLECTED IT FOR YOU!!

THIS ACT BURIED FOR GOOD BRITANNICUS' AMBITIONS. NERO READ THE DOCUMENT AND...

NONSENSE! FOOLISHNESS OF A SICK MIND!

47

...ND SO, THE SON DIED LIKE THE FATHER. HIS BODY WAS CARRIED ...UT OF THE ROOM. THE DEATH OF BRITANNICUS WAS THEATRICAL, ...ABRUPT, VIOLENT. BUT RUMORS STARTED TO SPREAD, TO GROW.

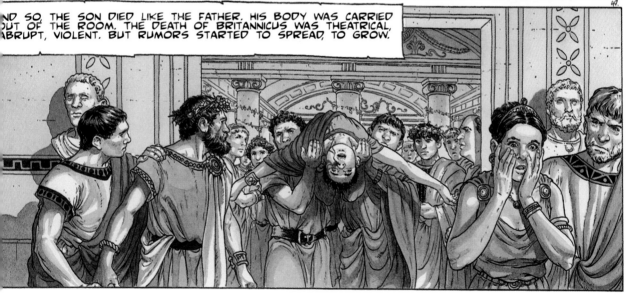

POISONING? BRITANNICUS WAS POISONED?

IT WOULD EXPLAIN HIS SUDDEN AND ATROCIOUS DEATH. AND THEN...(23)

AND THEN?

ONE OF OUR FRIENDS WHO DRANK FROM BRITANNICUS' CUP IS FEELING SICK, TOO.

YOUR FRIEND'S NAME?

TITUS FLAVIUS VESPASIAN-US(24).

A VIRTUOUS MAN. THERE IS NO REASON WHY I SHOULD NOT BELIEVE YOU. EVEN IF AS A MOTHER I SUFFER, I MUST PROSTRATE MY-SELF BEFORE SUCH FATAL EVIDENCE.

MAY MY DESCENT BE DAMNED...MY SON KILLED HIS BROTHER

I MUST BE ALONE IN MY SORROW.

HAH-HAH-HAH! MY SON, YOU WILL NEED YOUR MOTHER AGAIN. W ARE BOTH EATING THE SAME ROTTEN FRUIT CALLED POWER...

BUT MY MOUTH WILL BE MORE BITTER THAN YOURS.